For Katherine Walshe
with gratitude

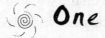

One

April 17th . . . Tuesday . . . 8.00 pm . . . This is day one
of the new me!!!!!

Oh but I love clean crisp pages, all blank and firm and
ready for me to write. I suppose that makes me a pretty sad
person. But you, new diary, are a big secret. Two days ago
I discovered that David, my grossly indecent almost fif-
teen-year-old brother had started to sneak into our room,
mine and Belle's, to read what I've written over the last
year and a bit. I hate him. I hate him because he's a low
life who I thought was trying to achieve something a bit
higher than his present sub-protozoan status. Wrong, so
wrong. For two reasons this makes me really angry: one,
the tissue-paper diary that he's tainted with his bitten fin-
gernails was given to me by Dad. It was a present and it
meant a lot. Second reason, I've had to store it away. It's

1

locked in a suitcase, which is locked in the loft; well, not locked – the loft is so chaotic that, were he to make his way up there and find it, he'd deserve a medal. I'm convinced his brain and his body are totally disconnected. Hopefully this time I'm on the winning side. I have to be.

I had to take my chances yesterday. Everybody was out, except for Jennifer-Mary. I stuck her in front of the television; Barney is a wonderful invention. She lay back like some beach babe, for once she did as she was told. Leaping upstairs like a crazed kangaroo I dragged the stepladder from behind the bathroom door. Why is everything broken in this house? Then I had to wedge the stepladder against the hot-press door. What crazy idiot put the roof space above the airing cupboard space? I don't know. This house was probably designed by a robot architect with extendable arms and legs. We've only lived here for a few years, but already the loft light flickers and dies and crackles like a weary volcano. And the dust, the dirt, the gross, close heat-smell up there was enough to make me want to puke. Yughhhh!!!!

By the time I got back downstairs Jenny-M was bored with Barney and had scattered a box of tissues from the TV room through to the kitchen. I happened to catch a glance of myself in the chrome bit of the cooker as I was clearing up after her. I was covered in streaks of dirt. Nice one, Jenny; occasionally you save my day. So, bathroom, ladder back exactly as I found it, quick face wash, clean hands. There is no way that I want Dave to know anything more. Creep!

I only hope that he doesn't know too much!

And now to you, new diary. Not a proper diary this time, a hardback copy, exactly like my science one; this'll fool him, camouflage by copyright! There is no way that he'll bother with what looks like a schoolbook. Dave doesn't think education is important. He thinks he's going to be spotted playing football and transported to England to become a superstar. Hopeless delusions of grandeur!!

Even before I write what I'm going to write I'm bursting. I'm excited, I'm thrilled. We did a poem today, by Keats. I love Keats. In a minute I'll look up which one it was, but it began . . .

'When I have fears that I may cease to be . . .'

Isn't that something else? Because I know that he was dead right to be fearful. Well, anyway, to me it's like a warning and a message. You, ordinary book, whose pages are easier to write on the right-hand side than the left, I'll try that and turn you upside down when I get to the end. Clear your head, Anna. This is a big moment. When I have fears that I may cease to be as excited and happy and hopeful.

I've done it. I can't believe it. I've finished and posted my novel, my first novel. I, Anna Elizabeth Sophie Fielding, have achieved a dream. Please let it be accepted. I'll go to church, dig the garden, wash the dishes, baby-sit for nothing, just as long as it's published. For all my life, all sixteen years of it, this is all I've wanted. To be a writer. Mum thinks it's brilliant. Dad tried to read it, but isn't heavily into stories; love stories, that is. Oh God, please don't let Andrew Butler know that he's the love interest. Why would he? Not unless dumb Dave is waiting like a virus to explode into action. Andrew is the brother of my friend Amy; he lives in England, he's working in Birmingham or somewhere, for an inner-city trust. Whatever that is. He's twenty-two and kind and tall and absolutely everything I want. But he's too old and he sees me as a little sister.

As I write that I can feel my heart pounding, just in case it gets shared with the wrong person. Sometimes families destroy faith. But no, I think this time I'm safe.

And now Mum's calling up the stairs, Amy's on the phone. I need an answering machine. Back later.

Here I am again, it's 8.47 and Amy wanted to know which pages of Biology we're meant to be studying for the exams. In a couple of months we're on holiday. I can't believe it. I'd better sort my head out or I'm going to fail everything. I think I was a bit rushed with Amy. She understands. I couldn't explain the urgency, not with everyone around. Dad's in the kitchen making coffee, the phone's on the wall right next to the kettle. Mum's trying to stuff the washing machine, get Jen ready for bed, persuade Dave to do his homework, Belle to sort her precious clothes from the rest that can be jammed in with the jeans. Terry was in the sitting room reading a computer manual, disturbing nobody.

'Terry, get in here and help your mother!' Dad yelled. Terry looked mightily impressed gazing down at Belle's new underwear, Dave's soccer gear and assorted shirts and towels and face cloths and just about everything we all wear and own. I don't think that Maeve Binchy and Deirdre Purcell and Danielle Steel, never mind Roddie Doyle, have my problems. BUT. . . this is the new positive me. I've promised myself. I need to write everything down, right now before Belle comes upstairs, because once she hits the bedroom I can't think, between hair spray and body spray. Belle's created her own personal gap in the ozone layer. Forget conferences in Rio, we ought to hold one right here in this house. Now. Deep breath. Where was I?

I've called my novel 'The Jacob Dream'. The main characters are Jacob, he's a doctor, and Tina, she's a student nurse. I learned quite a bit about hospitals a few years ago. I had meningitis and spent what felt like years getting better. While I was there I met this brilliant nurse, her name was Clodagh, she's living somewhere exotic; once it was Australia but the last postcard she sent was from Taiwan. She definitely won't recognise herself. I've made the Tina character overweight. Well, she thinks she's overweight, she isn't really. Anyway, as the book progresses and romance blossoms, she turns into this incredibly elegant and stunning woman. Kind of the opposite of me. That's why being a writer is so fantastic. You can be anybody.

Sally, Amy and Andrew's mum, typed it up for me. I respect Sally and asked her opinion. She was a bit hesitant, muttered something about not being too disappointed if a few changes had to be made. I can do that. Anyway, it's not really her kind of thing, either. She tends to read biographies and histories. My book is in the post, winging its way to Conroy International. Their address was in a magazine my sister Belle reads. I'll try to describe the famous Belle. She's fourteen, blonde, bossy and, so everybody tells me, beautiful. Who am I to judge? All right, if I'm honest with myself she's pretty. Pretty what, I haven't quite worked out. She's turned herself into Blondie Spice over the last six months. She was watching some early-morning chat show or other and claims to be their original fan. Good luck to her. And I think I'm pathetic!

My brother David, as I said, almost fifteen, unremarkable but for the smell of his feet and the size of his ego which could fill a hot-air balloon, is another member of the Spice rack; his reasons are unsubtly different. Dave has achieved dirty-old-man status before his sixteenth birthday. I told Mum that he ought to be taken to a sex therapist. She told me that he was full of hormones. That information I did not want to know or digest. Terry – there's nine months between us – is definitely not like Dave, even if they do share the same parents. I sometimes bless the fact that I'm adopted; at least all the worst bits about Dave and our almost three-year-old sister Jennifer-Mary won't corrupt me, I hope. Then again, maybe it is the background not the genes that makes you a gross, four-letter-word-using, thumb-sucking, snoring, anti-social, graceless bore. No. Can't be. I'm not like that!

It's like starting again, diary. I'm Anna. I live in Temple Manor Park, Baltinogar, County Cork. I'm kind of thrilled, in between being mortified and angry. Maybe starting again wasn't such a bad idea after all. As from today a different life has begun. I'm a writer. A real writer. I've written a book. Me, all dream and ambition. A book. Stop there. Go into reverse. Just in case you read this in twenty years time. Jesus – no, sorry, that's blasphemy. No it isn't, I mean it. THIS diary is my real book, my real story, real me, not Jacob and Tina, not the me who has to keep quiet, say sorry when I want to tell someone they're crude and cruel. But I don't want to read anything about me so far away in the future. Then again, maybe it could come in handy.

Time to go. I can hear Belle and Dave arguing at the bottom of the stairs. I don't care. Today's the beginning of my future. Isn't it?

TWO

Don't count the pages, this is a second entry. It's Wednesday, a half day, meant to be for sports. I'm useless at just about everything to do with a racquet or a ball or my legs, which seem to run one way and twist another. Truth. I hate to be told to be sporty. But, that's why I like Wednesday. I get my own free time. Friday's another good day, there's the weekend to look forward to, maybe a lie-in. But right now it's 2.30 and sunny and Terry and his friends are messing with the internet at school. Amy asked me if I wanted to join them. No thank you. No. I'm trying to get my head round the book, the family, this house. Everything. Not only Jacob and Tina but . . .

Mum's gone shopping with Belle, who's looking for something new to wear at the disco on Saturday. Why does she bother? At this stage she knows everybody who lives here, has visited here, or might visit here. I don't want to know where Dave is. And Jen is safely (I hope) asleep in her bed. It's a disaster putting that kid in a bed. I told the parents, tie her in her cot until she's old enough to know better than wander the house in the early hours of the morning. It's terrifying. You wake up in the middle of the night and you know something is out there, watching you. It's Jen. Head height to bed height, waiting. Not saying anything, she's all damp and clammy in your mind, half sleeping. She's looking at you in the moonlight, probably one of the undead and Mum and Dad haven't noticed the puncture marks on her neck. I'll check next time she's awake.

Anyway, back to me. Where are you, Anna? I think I'm kind of splitting my personality with sheer joy. Why? Because I'm almost alone and I feel peaceful and excited at the same time. I've got to get back to earth. I'm in our bedroom. I can hear the television. Normal. I can hear music. What's new? Nothing gets turned off in this place. Now I can hear Jenny-M singing in bed. Please stay singing for a while longer. I can smell chips, lunchtime chips.

I need a beginning for this new diary/journal. Not right at the start, the adoption and all that, something new. OK. Here goes. When transition year began in September I was dreading it. I wanted to get going, get on with my Leaving, apply to college, begin the real thing, not some dumb practice session. Big surprise, most of it isn't too bad. Initially, I decided that whoever had had the bright idea of being transited lacked a sense of humour and was probably a freak cynic who thought adding a year onto school was a good enough punishment for anyone under twenty. But, with a new head teacher – in fact, my old English teacher, Mr. Finbar Kennedy – things really have improved. According to Mum he's quite young. I hope I never know what being on the other side of forty looks like. Mr. Kennedy is no babe. Still, he's not so bad in a boring kind of way and some of the promises of going to the theatre and visiting factories and meeting writers and scientists, etc., etc., materialised. I did my work experience in the kitchens of The Blackthorn Stop, a very smart hotel on the outskirts of the city. Getting there was a nightmare; for buses read bus. If you missed the 7.45 in the morning then it was thumbing it or praying someone you knew was passing. I won't describe the kitchen experience; if half the guests knew what went on in there they'd sign themselves into a clinic. Mum got me the job, she knows the housekeeper. Why doesn't she know the manager of the Opera House, or chief sales-person of HMV? I might have enjoyed that. My kitchen skills are limited, and doubly so when the heat and steam and noise and shouting fill your head to bursting. And I didn't get paid. According to the chef, eating his leftovers was treat enough. HUH!!!

We took a trip round the university. It was March and freezing. I made a mental note to start saving for a fur coat and large hat. There was so much to see. I wished that I was actually there as a student, not a silly schoolgirl in uniform. Everybody seemed to know where they were going. I don't know how, but Amy, Ruth, another friend and I got lost. We were looking at a sculpture for a moment. Then, lost. We spent what felt like hours wandering chilly stone corridors trying to find the rest of our party. Ruth has this ability to strike up conversations with anyone, any age. She found herself a stunning-looking guy, leather satchel swung casually from his shoulder, huge scarf wrapped round his neck, really cool glasses. I sometimes wish that I wore glasses, they'd look good when I'm being interviewed, make me look more intellectual. Anyway, Ruth stood, looking adorable, just about reaching his shoulder, asking the way. It's at moments like that that I consider having a few inches taken off my height. I'm five foot ten. Don't believe all those short people who tell you height is wonderful. It's a scam, a dirty scheme, they're all laughing behind your back, your very long back. Because they are the ones who can buy shirts and jeans and skirts and dresses without having to have bits added on. I suffer from perpetually cold wrists because all those shop buyers are maximum five foot six and don't know that all the other people like me need a bit of extra material.

I digress. I do it all the time. Mr. Spectacular put us on the right road. We found everyone in this big dining area. I felt like a fish in a bowl. The real students muttered and mumbled as we were given watered-down orange squash and ham and cheese sandwiches. I was starving, so I ate. But I longed to rush the months forward, to be a part of all that activity.

Two wishes. Please, please let my book be published.
And let me be older soon. Now a third one. Let me be
honest to this diary. It's important.

✺ Three

April 28th ... Saturday ... 10.45 am ... Sorry diary. No entries. All I've done is revise, lose my art project and have a major fall-out with Ruth who's decided to have her belly button pierced. Why? I hate the word belly, it conjures up ugly images. Ruth said it, I grimaced. Then she said she needs to have it done. Needs to? Why? What's next? I know what's next, all her smart Dublin friends have uniformly decided that where there's a flap there has to be a stud, a ring, a pole. DO NOT WANT TO THINK ABOUT IT.

Anyway, it's a week and three days since I posted my book. I'm having doubts. Ruth read it and said she thought I was being over-ambitious. What does that mean? No, I haven't been to all the brilliant places that she has because there's only one of her and five of us. Plus her father is super rich and her mother is super chic. Good word chic. What exactly is wrong with it, the book? My book.

Amy's going to be here in a minute, there's a new family moving in and we thought we'd have a quick look. Who knows, they might be exciting. Doubt it, Temple Manor Park is hardly Sin City. When we first moved here and it was just us lot and very superior neighbours next door, I hated the place. Now, all of a sudden, there's a mad rush to fill the vacant plots. Our dog, Fernando, is perpetually getting into trouble. He got used to the wide open spaces, but now he's being dragged back by strangers demanding that we keep him chained up. About eight houses away there's this new couple, Kerry and Margaret McCarthy; they have two little children, Adam, 3, and Chloe, 1. They're useful in one respect because they pay me to baby-sit, but they're scary in another, because she, Margaret, the mother, is a health freak. She reckons that Fernando is a walking toxic bomb. I know that he doesn't smell that great – if I'm being honest he smells terrible – but I don't believe that we've been living for the past five years with a designer creature from some secret laboratory. She gave Mum all this literature on Toxicaria. Poor Mum was so embarrassed.

'It's in the faeces,' Margaret kept saying.

Jenny-M, who is heavily into mimicking whatever anyone else says, got the wrong end of the word and began to shout 'feckeez, feckeez'. Mum was turning white and grey into a new shade of oatmeal, Margaret had covered Adam's ears, and Jenny, in command centre-stage, shouted this brand new word even louder.

It's poor old Fernando who's the loser. He stands with his paws against the window ledge barking and growling and occasionally escaping. Maybe we ought to find him a new home. I found him the other day pathetically scratching at Bimbo the dead cat's grave. Poor old Bimbo. She was seventeen, which, as the vet said, was a great age. Jenny-M found her. Bimbo was lying on a blanket in the kitchen, completely stiff. Dad said it was a nice way to go. Jenny lugged her upstairs, which is kind of macabre when you analyse it closely, but I don't think analysis will ever be one of Jen's strong points.

'Pussy's cold,' she announced, dumping the corpse between the sleeping parents.

I can't describe the hysterics, the tears, the drama, because most of it was down to me. I liked that cat. Any-way, I've dissuaded Fernando from digging up his old buddy by putting mesh over her one-time favourite sun-ning spot. It'd be too Stephen King to have him dragging her back indoors. But, then again, anything is possible.

The door bell. Great. Amy's here. More later. Oh but I'm a genius to keep two diaries. Eat your little heart out, Dave. This one you'll never find and the other is snug and warm and away from your prying paws.

11.30 pm. Well. What a let-down! Amy's staying and Belle has gone to her mate Shazza, beloved Sheherazade, twin to Toby and daughter of Dora. No comment. Dora is magnetically attracted to my mother because Mum's altogether too patient with her. But what a disappointment the new people are! He's a hundred if he's a day, she's ninety, and they are WEIRD. He has white hair and wears sandals, with socks! She also has white hair and talks to birds (no, not female humans, the sort that fly, the kind that steal the strawberries and leave large amounts of disgusting white stuff on the windscreen of the car).

'Come on, my pets. Come on down.'

Amy and I looked at each other as we pretended to be going somewhere just as the removal van was being unloaded. I've decided he's a retired spy, the amount of computer screens and disk boxes that were being carried indoors. And what Temple Manor has are not pets, they are dirty great crows who dive-bomb for food and who screech and squawk from about four in the morning during summer. I like animals, hence the big tragedy scene over the cat. But birds. God made them fly for a reason, to keep them out of my way.

We can see their garden from Mum and Dad's bedroom, so we kept a close eye on the proceedings as a large concrete bird table was being erected. This thing looks like a satellite dish capable of keeping them in touch with the Kremlin. What do they expect to land on it? Ostriches, Storks? Just our luck! We now have a resident health fascist, plus embryonic house Martians.

Amy wants to talk. Terry is staying over at his mate Frag's. Dave? Hopefully he's in the middle of a terrible dream. And I must keep a close eye on those new people;

16

I'm probably living on top of the scoop of the century. If only they'd been younger, normal, accompanied by three sons and a couple of interesting daughters. Goodnight.

✺ Four

Monday is over. Monday was dull. French, first class, Ms. 'don't-call-me-Mrs.' Wolfe. I wouldn't call her anything but a terrible teacher. She thinks that she's brilliant. Brilliant . . . Now there's a thought. What she is is a bully. How do you tell family, friends and dozey teachers that, instead of waiting around at break time to see the part-time extortionists at work – the junior members of the fraternity, the students – look instead inside the staff room. I'm into women working, that's exactly what I intend to do, but take a break, really take a break, and have a look at the true bullies. They are not bruisers and bouncers. They are nice and kind during parents' day and polite when talking during assembly, but some of the teachers in this school give our sex a bad name. They can't all be menopausal and, even if they are, some of them have to have read *Hello, She, Cosmo*. HRT. Hormone Replacement Therapy. If I've read about it, why haven't they? I'll tell you why. They are not nice people. Ms. Wolfe, for example; her husband's a surgeon. I have nothing against surgeons, good folk, a bit scissor and stitch happy, but good. Well, he's probably working sixteen-hour days to pay for her soft top car (it's a cute little thing which should be driven by Andrew or someone like him). However, he, Mr. 'don't-call-me-Dr.' Wolfe, probably comes home knackered.

'How was your day, dear?' he asks, all silenced by the plush velvet of the chairs and curtains and carpets.

'Terrible, darling. I had to cope with those transition years. They're so inferior, so stupid. I should be in a lovely convent school in Bray, or Cannes, or Monaco . . .'

'Oh, darling.' Imagine the glug, glug, of the brandy into a Waterford cut glass.

'Relax. You're too good for them.'

She, Ms. Wolfe, has forgotten to mark our homework for three weeks and he's pouring her brandy and planning a summer break in Tuscany.

She's not the only one. Boys in particular confuse and upset Ms. Halpern. Ms. Halpern teaches Maths and Geography. She's nice enough if you like faded lace curtains and spiders for friends. But boys, adolescent, spotty, sometimes rather mouthy males, really upset her.

'Get up here,' she commanded Terry this morning.

Terry is almost the same height as me. As brothers go, he is the exception to the rule. Terry is a pet. No, bad word, Terry is shy and hesitant and brings out the better side of my nature. (According to Mum that is. She's forever telling me to be nicer to Belle and Dave and Jenny-M. She had them; her problem not mine.)

Anyway, Terry went up the length of the classroom. Because he was concentrating so hard on not going red and banging into desks and all the inglorious things one does when you know that you're in trouble and you don't know why, he tripped over a discarded schoolbag. Of course he did. It was inevitable. Didn't Ms. Halpern ever do something like that? Probably not, she was probably born boring and has worked her way into being terribly boring since that first horrifying moment she hit this earth.

'You found that amusing, I suppose?'

How could she think that? Hasn't she read his personal history notes? Before you get signed into our school the adult in your life has to answer a million and one questions about who you are, where you lie buried in the family, what state you are in physically and emotionally. Locked away is a very personal X file that somebody must have access to.

'Well?' Halpern spat.

He couldn't speak. Like Billy Budd, he goes silent. He goes dumb.

'You were talking over my voice.'

Not easy; she could be used by every airport and train station simultaneously to do the announcements. Her voice doesn't grate it serrates. Horrible.

'Well?'

Terry wasn't well, he was terrified. So I stood up.

'Sit down.'

I stayed standing. We both ended up outside the headmaster's office.

'You two. Again,' Ms. Wolfe sneered, breezing out with a sheaf of papers.

It was all right in the end. Terry had calmed down enough to be able to explain that he was giving his log book to Frag, Francis Gregory, Terry's best friend. We both got a detention, which is a pain because we'll have to wait an extra half hour for the bus home. But, at least I tried to get my point across to Mr. Kennedy that occasionally teachers could try backing off.

'Don't be vulgar.' He sounded pained. I want to know why he didn't go to a speech therapist and learn to pronounce his 'r's and 'th's. Mum has threatened to make me share a room with Belle and Shazza for a whole week if I dare to ask that particular question.

'He's a lovely man.'

She has to say that, he's on all sorts of local committees with my father. Dad, Robert, Bob to his friends.

I'm wanted downstairs. By the time I'm old and grey I'll have written the biggest collection of odes dedicated to mashing potatoes, stirring gravy and tipping slops into the dog's bowl. I NEED INSPIRATION.

It's 9.30 pm . . . Everyone's downstairs watching a video. I'm supposed to be having a bath. Later.

Still no word about my book. I wanted to ring, but,

seeing as the publishers are in York, I didn't think that was such a good idea. Dad has recently acquired a mobile phone. Anyone would think he'd just been recruited by MI5. It's like it's meant to be a big secret. We all know that he keeps it in the top pocket of his overalls. We all know that it's expensive to use. We'd all love to have one of our own.

'If I see any one of you using it, there'll be trouble.'

Yawn. A while back we went through group family therapy sessions. I'm convinced it's made me psychologically obsessed. But sometimes Dad remembers the listening bit, the liking your children bit, the giving your wife space bit. But on the whole he's regressed pretty rapidly. Getting to know his brother Sean, our Uncle Sean, explained a lot.

In a normal family you'd know if you had relatives. Wouldn't you? Not in ours, despite the best help from Matt the psychologist. We were all led to believe that Mum and Dad were only children, just them, singletons. I'm the exception, of course. I could have parents with twelve brothers and sisters each, but I was ditched in the Good Faith Adoption Agency when I was a few days, or a few weeks old, what's the difference. Anyway, there'd been whispers of Sean's existence but over the years he got kind of lost in family mists and silences.

It doesn't matter. Last June this very pleasant American man arrived at the front door. Mum was out, Jen was sleeping and I was taking care of her, because that's what I do. Belle was socialising, because that's what she does, and Terry and Dave were probably arguing over the computer.

'Hi. Bob around?'

Nice image, bobbing around.

'No. Sorry. Dad's at work.'

Dad works and works; his proper job is managing a cycle shop and when he's not 'at work' he works some more at home.

'My name's Sean. I suppose I'm your uncle.'

!!!!!!!!!!

He lives in the States, Oregon. He's in Manpower Services. How come everyone has these jobs with big descriptions and you haven't the slightest notion of what they do? I understand teacher, doctor, solicitor, hopefully publisher. But Manpower Services?!!! Anyway, after the parents got over the shock and we got over having someone around who handed ten pound notes to us like twenty pence pieces, we all got on; kind of. He stayed for three weeks. It was just about the time that I was able to say Bimbo's name without bursting into tears. I hated that mourning time, I honestly didn't think that a cat could have crept so close to my soul. What if it were a person? How would you cope? Anyway, Sean and I had a heart-to-heart in the garden. The sun was shining, Dad and I had almost completed a blazing row because I had categorically refused to help Mum sort out the boys' bedroom.

'Wait till they get back from town and make them do it. It's their room, their responsibility.'

You don't want to hear the details. Mum cried

23

because I was getting cross, Dad yelled because he knew I was right. I assume that he knew I was right. And Uncle Sean motioned to me with two cans of Coke in his hand. God it was great, we had ice cream in the freezer, which stayed frozen because Sean insisted on buying the parents a new fridge.

'For your hospitality.' He informed them as it was being unloaded.

They weren't hospitable; well, I suppose Mum was, but Dad tended to be spittable.

'Your Dad's got a lot to think about,' he explained, all too obviously, as we settled on the two loungers he and I had purchased the day before from a DIY place. Shopping, this man could give seminars on the subject.

'Would it have hurt so much to help your Mum?'

I explained the principle of the thing. He's one of the easiest guys to talk to. Seeing as I didn't even know that he existed, he and I got on pretty well.

'Sometimes it's worth burying the odd highly-strung principle. Take Bob for example.'

No thank you, you can have him. He's all yours.

'I'm eight years his junior.'

It shows. How come Dad is bald and Sean isn't? And who out of Dave and Terry will go bald? I worry. Terry has soft brown hair. Dave's is long, tied back with a shoelace. He's got an earring which he insists on wearing all the time. He spends his life getting notes from school. If he had his way he'd probably have tattooed across his face, 'I hate authority'.

Sean really tried to get me on Dad's side. Why? He knew that the parents hadn't told us about him. But he bothered. I admire that.

'Being eight years younger than your dad meant that I had a much easier time when it came to school. Our parents could afford all the books, the blazer, the pen, with ink. Bob never had any of that. Anyway, after college – remember, I went to college after I left for the States, and after I'd saved and bought the house – well, I wrote to your dad and said I'd like to repay his kindness to me when I was young. He worked hard, gave half his money to Daddy and Mammy when they were alive. He didn't reply for a long while. When he did, he refused my offer. It had been a matter of principle being the eldest, to help in my support. It was not necessary for me to repay him. I wasn't. Don't get principles and pride and pig-headedness in your way, Anna. You can be terribly like your dad, you know.'

I was going to point out that, given we were not slightly related, this was an accidental slip of the tongue. But there was something kind of haunted in the way Uncle Sean said it. He never married. The parents explained this to us after he left; they had dark expressions on their faces. So? But he did have a good friend. Big deal! I don't know why they don't just accept him for what he is: generous, considerate and very rich. I think the rich could come in rather handy.

This family has secrets. What for? I hate secrets. You, diary, are not a secret, you're a record, that's different. In the unlikely event that I ever have children, I'm going to tell them everything. What's the point in hiding a brother who just happens not to agree with the way you lead your life. Every card Sean had sent over the long years had been chucked out. Didn't they know that eventually he'd want to meet us? Arrogance, that's what it was, sheer high-mindedness. We all liked Sean. He wants Terry to go out there some time after he's finished school to see if he'd like to go to college in the States. Dad was silent. Mum was cautious. Terry was thrilled. He's a genius with electronic things, computers and all the sort of stuff that I manage to break or fuse. It would take a big weight off Mum and Dad. But no. Unless a miracle happens, Terry will not be going. I don't understand.

These days my brain is constantly fixed on the whereabouts of Jacob and Tina. I leap downstairs, I pray for a letter, a cheque would be nice. Nothing. Plenty of bills. A demand from the school requiring an explanation at the parents' convenience for Dave's absences. That really got to Mum. They have to go in and see the head about him. Dad, of course, is far too busy.

'But Bob. We need to discuss this.'

No reply. No discussion. Things are not good on the parent front. I feel sick thinking about it. Tomorrow I'm going to have to talk to someone. Goodnight. I must have a bath before Baltinogar's answer to a beauty queen swans up the stairs. And if she doesn't stop her soft spluttery snoring when she falls asleep I'm going to sticky-tape her mouth shut.

꩜ Five

Wednesday May 2nd ... *another half day. I should be* studying. Exams begin too soon. I feel haunted and empty. At least this time not everything depends on them. I hated the Junior Cert. Feeling sick twenty-four hours a day, going to sleep knowing that you've forgotten just about everything you've learnt. One of the girls in class gained over a stone in weight. She's in a recovery centre some-where suffering from Bulimia. I wish that everything didn't depend on the Leaving. Thinking about this year, almost a wasted year in some ways, makes me feel my veins are going to erupt and my brain explode. No. I refuse to contemplate all this. Poor old Terry spent most of the month of last June looking like a very poorly corpse. Meanwhile Ruth sailed through all of it. How? Because it doesn't matter. Her family will get her 'in' somewhere, or attached to some multinational or other. It's so unjust.

Terry and I ended up with almost identical results. Being in the same class is good because we study together. Well, almost the same results. I didn't exactly pass Irish and German and he only scraped English. I don't know why, his vocabulary's better than mine, he just doesn't know how to use it.

I've been keeping a close eye on the new neighbours. Fernando did one of his mad-dash escapes the other day. The old man was stroking him lovingly as I raced up to their new garden gate. We've had a police threat from Margaret. She told Mum that if we couldn't control the dog then we ought to be relieved of him. I told her that that was an infringement of liberty and she snapped back that had I read all the pamphlets I would understand that the welfare of her children was more important than any sentimental attachment. I could have smacked her, she's so smug, so right. He doesn't do any harm. Anyway the old man said Fernando was a beautiful animal. I'm sure I'm right, he has to be a spy or something odd, he has a foreign – for foreign read continental – accent. I don't know where his wife was. Fernando and he really got on. He can't be too bad.

This morning there was blossom floating everywhere. The car was like a bridal bus. It looked as if overnight some kind fairy had ditched the dust and exchanged it for petals. Dad called Mum out to see it. Why can't there be nice moments twenty-four hours a day? Jen was allowed to help clear the windscreen by collecting all the different shades of pink in a lace bag. MY FIRST COMMUNION BAG, mother! I didn't mind. I keep reminding myself that I've got to store up images. Jilly Cooper does that, makes notes about clouds and rain and the seasons. I'd probably lose mine, or the dog would eat them, or Mum would throw them out when she has one of her rare cleaning rushes. Oh for a lap-top computer. I wouldn't know how to use it, but I'd learn.

I tried talking to Ms. Spillane; she used to teach Terry and I history. Brief explanation, just in case this is being read by a researcher in the year two thousand and forty. Now I feel spacey. There's a gap in my stomach, thinking about the future or forever, it does that to you. It's like wondering about whom you might marry. He's out there, living his life, being brought up (or down) by his family. And one day, you meet. What does that feel like? How do you know? Do you know? Too much. I'm going to go downstairs and get a glass of milk. I sometimes wish I didn't think.

6.45 pm . . . Usually we all watch *Home and Away*. It's a Fielding family thing and it's consistent. Not tonight. Talk about atmosphere. It's boiling hot outside. I know, I know, unusual for Cork. But it is. Inside the kitchen it's below freezing. Dad, Mum and Dave are sitting in there, silent as I bashed about looking for a glass, a bottle of something more interesting than Jen's vitamin-enriched juice. Naturally Dave has drunk all the good stuff. All the tea things are sitting there, unwashed. I offered to clear away.

'No thank you.' Mum sounded like a voice with a

mission. Definitely not Mother Theresa, more Pol Pot. Disentangling myself from the dog who wanted to lick my bare feet – Fernando likes flesh – I suggested a sandwich, toast, anything to break the silence and the sobs. Dave had been crying. I wanted to help. Mum had this hard line of a mouth about her. She rarely looks angry, but this was real.

'Be quick, Anna,' she snapped.

'Do you want anything, Dave?' I asked.

'You heard your mother.'

Yes thank you father. Loud and clear. As I closed the door I heard Dad saying, 'What you need is a good belting.'

Great.

Mum will plead, Dad will threaten, then it'll all get forgotten, because that's what we do in this place; move halfway towards a solution and then pull back. It's as if there's something stopping us from changing. Dave hates school. Not your average hates school, this is a diabolical loathing. I think he probably should go to another place. There's a brand new one about to be finished for September term. Dave needs to start again. Yes he's a spoilt, insolent, loud-mouthed pervert, but he's also pathetically under the thumb of his friends. Dave is the big man, or so he thinks, in his group. He makes them laugh, he's the class clown. The teachers loathe him, and his friends laugh at him. He gets caught, they get a giggle. I'll talk to Mum tomorrow. Dad wants him to stay because he knows a lot of the teachers and the parents and I suppose thinks that they'll do him some special favour. Baltinogar is a very small place, even if it's growing. But nobody is going to do any favours for Dave. I might even try talking to Dave tomorrow. That'd be a first.

I'm in the bathroom now. It's after eleven and Dave's been in his room for about an hour. Terry and he have been locked away, no music, nothing. Very strange. I knocked on the door but Terry said to go away. It hurt; normally it's him and me against the Fielding conspiracy. Maybe they'll talk, sort something out.

Belle has just asked me why I'm constantly writing up science notes. Give the girl an A+, she actually noticed I exist. Normally she's so caught up with blue nail varnish and champagne streaks in her luscious locks, she tends to treat me like worn-out mascara. I'm too tired. A million moths are floating between my stomach and my chest. The bathroom floor is sopping wet. Thank you, Belle. There's a whirring and a whining coming from the loft. It sounds as if a family of mice are locked in there working on electric sewing machines. I ought to mention it to Dad, then again I'd better not; he'd think that I want him to do something about the noise.

'Doesn't anyone else in this place do anything?' he moans.

What can you say? He, poor old Dad, is determined to suffer. I hear footsteps. Too late . . .

'Yes. All right. I'll turn off the light.'

Find me an alien, instantly. I WANT to be beamed up. Where are the UFOs when you need them?

31

Six

Revision, revision, revision. Ms. Spillane asked me to come and have a chat with her during break. I re-read what I wrote yesterday; I still haven't explained exactly who Ms. Spillane is.

'How did you get on last night?' she asked.

I tried to tell her that things were not that easy last night. She teaches History and Irish; she is one heavy-duty Irish speaker. When the family were going through their last breakdown she was really helpful. Mum and she get on, but, because of this, I don't think that she wants to be seen as interfering. Interfere away. I want to tell her everything. But I won't.

I spoke to Mum about the new school that Dave might transfer to. She was hard and silent; she carried on scrubbing at the remains of scrambled egg at the bottom of a once non-stick pan. Dad had left, no goodbye, no petals to be collected and wondered at. Dave has definitely upset them. I tried to ask her about Dad. I know how annoyed he can get but lately it's been more than annoyed. Mum told me to leave him alone, that he has too many problems of his own to fix. Hello, is anybody listening? We need fixing. Dad's boss, Mr. Arthur O'Conor, is downsizing. What a word, what a world. What Mr. Arthur O'Conor is doing is selling off his businesses. Two of my schoolmates have lost their part-time jobs in one of his video stores. He wasn't exactly paying them much, one forty an hour isn't a bank breaker, but . . .

Terry's really worried about Dave. They were up talking until four this morning. You could tell; the pair of them looked like Frankenstein's assistants. I smiled at Dave over the cornflakes and a look of absolute terror crossed his face. I tried to tell him that I wasn't getting at him, that I genuinely understood. He leapt up, grabbed his bag, forgot his lunch and ran for it. I think I'd better start working on my people skills. Sally says that's why we're better off in families, that way we get to work out all the wrinkles in our relationships before we take to the road as independents. Maybe she's right.

Drama. Belle has a spot. I haven't got room for spots because I have freckles. I get rashes. This sun thing is not good for the likes of me. Amy and I were put together for tennis this afternoon. Think David and Goliath. She fell, so we had to go to the school secretary to get disinfectant and a plaster. Ms. Wolfe was in there. The door was open.

33

'I wish the whole family would move on. There was all that scandal about the brother and now that lout . . .'

Her eyebrow was raised in a nasty plucked arch. It stayed up there as I helped the hobbling Amy in. There was silence. I couldn't speak. The wolf turned on her open-toed sandals, her yellowy toe-nails peaking through. Roald Dahl, you were right, there are witches.

Later I went back to Amy's. Sally's been having treatment for a slipped disc. Normally she's leaping around, talking all the time. A lot of people find her strange; in other words she doesn't do or say what they do. But today she was quiet, pensive. We made her a cup of tea.

'This damn back!' she cried out, trying to get comfortable.

You could see that she was in pain, real live trapped pain.

'All I do is watch television. Holding up a book hurts.'

The old Sally would have asked about 'The Jacob Dream', the new version didn't even seem that interested when I told her about Ms. Wolfe. But then, as I was leaving, she apologised.

'Sorry, Anna. I'm scared. I've been recommended an operation and I'm scared.'

I wanted to give her a hug. I suppose I should have.

'Don't worry about Pat Wolfe. She's forgotten that her mother and father ran the post office. Apparently they were really good people. She and your dad know all about each other. That's all.'

That's all!!!!!!!!!!!!!!! It's Thursday May 3rd . . . I'm surrounded by conspiracies. Dave had his tea and slouched off like a beaten animal. Dad sat and mopped up egg juice in silence. Mum looks as if she's been told that she mightn't wake up tomorrow. Belle, wisely, was absent. If she bothered to read a book then I suppose she'd have read Edgar Allen Poe and decided she needed a break from Gothic horror. Terry excused himself and disappeared. Even Jen sensed the occasion; she silently fed Fernando large chunks of bread and butter and snugged herself and her quilt and her monkey on the couch in the TV room and fell asleep.

I promised myself positive, diary. Sometimes it isn't easy.

꩜ Seven.

Saturday . . . May 5th . . . 3.14 pm.

Help! Only two days to the start of the exams. I love 'The Plough and the Stars' but I don't know any quotes and I seem to like all the wrong characters. I think Nora's a pain and Bessie Burgess is brilliant. Our new English teacher, Mr. Rose, has to be a secret Mills and Boon writer in his spare time. All his talk of star-crossed lovers and flint and foam relationships give me a headache. Start him off on Cathy and Heathcliff and he almost melts in front of us. He ought to be forced to sit in on our family. Reality doesn't only bite, it amputates.

Mum's visit to Mr. Kennedy was humiliating and excruciating. He suggested that perhaps Dave would be better placed in another school, after he's been assessed by an educational psychologist. It's so unfair; he seemed to have made Mum out to be an awful parent. She isn't. And how would he know, he doesn't even have any children. All he's doing is scooping out a failure, somebody who needs help, and then tossing him like a bit of gristle onto a scrap heap.

I was listening as Mum talked to Dad about it. Sometimes not having a dishwasher pays off. Seeing as they won't discuss anything with us directly, we're forced to eavesdrop. Terry was fiddling with the innards of mum's little kitchen radio which she's owned since she was fifteen. It's showing definite signs of wear and tear, a bit like her.

Terry and I cornered Dave, who's broken out in the worst case of acne I've ever seen. He should be studying. He says he can't. He should be trying to persuade everyone that he's not a messer, that he can behave. He says he doesn't know how.

'Why don't you try St. Stephen's then?' Terry, pacing, looking at Dave eye to eye, suggested.

'I won't know anyone. They're all going to be scuts and drop-outs,' was Dave's response.

I had to clamp my teeth on my tongue to prevent my saying: a bit like you. But I didn't. And he's thinking about it, St. Stephens. 'I'll help you if you want to revise,' I offered.

This is a big sacrifice.

'Why would you bother?' He snarled.

'We both will,' Terry the peacemaker, sensing that I was not necessarily going to maintain my temper, intervened.

A four-letter word later, with a couple of others added on, ended this sibling exchange. Now there's an idea. Let's swap Dave for someone peaceful. I don't mean that. I don't hate him, I just don't know how to get to the bottom of his problem.

5.00 pm . . . Shazza's here, Toby's here. Help. I want to be anywhere but here. Dora and Tom Hennessy, the parents, are taking a little trip to London. Dora tends to use the word 'little' a lot. 'You know that nice little woman in number three,' she'll say. I can sense an unsheathed claw when I feel one. What she really means is that cheaply dressed, downtrodden, quite obviously inferior to me, the dynamic Dora, little woman. Dora and I do not get on. In fact Dora thinks I'm from bad stock. You can sense that she believes that babies like me should have been left on a handy mountainside and fed to the foxes.

7.15 pm . . . Heaven. Orange juice, fresh; cheesecake, delicious.

An interruption. I'm now resting on a very comfortable couch in Margaret and Kerry McCarthy's sitting room. Baby-sitting bliss. My homework is spread in front of me. Later. Can't handle homework at this minute. I've read fourteen Mr. Men stories to Adam and Chloe, who are now safely tucked in their beds. Why doesn't Jennifer-M do as she's told? Spoilt, that's why. She almost died, which I suppose doesn't exactly inspire confidence in the average parent.

This room is definitely bigger than ours. I can see out to all the older children playing on the grass. If they wake Chloe and Adam I'll scalp the lot of them. I have plans, television plans. Help!! Fernando's out there too. More trouble.

11.00 pm ... Strange. I'm back in our room. Belle is absorbing an end of Cannes interview with her girl-power favourites. No, that's not what's strange. Margaret and Kerry came back very early and very silent. Usually they're like love's young dream, all kisses on the doorstep and sweet smiles. We had them round here as soon as they moved in. No need for a neighbourhood watch, just ask Mum. Anyway, they could hardly keep their hands off each other. Poor old Chloe and Adam. But tonight it was a fiver in my hand, a bang of the front door and what sounded like Prince Nasseem taking on the Celtic warrior.

Kerry's a publishing agent. Useful? Forget it. He's only interested in photographers and artists. I tried asking him a few questions. But he explained that he was running the Cork office of a much bigger concern in Dublin. So what? He informed me he was here to scoop the talent, then he'd move on. I thought they'd bought their house. No, they're renting it. Guess who owns it? Yes, and yes again. Our dearly beloved benefactor, Arthur on-your-bike O'Conor. So that's why he's selling up and moving everyone out. He's decided to invest in property. Don't you hate that? I'm tired. Please let me remember something on Monday apart from my own name.

Eight

Sunday May 6th ... I've left my watch downstairs. No idea what time it is.

Dad was in another foul mood this morning. He hates Saturdays, he has to work, but to make him go in on a Sunday is too much. Call it intuition or my being dramatic, I sense something dark and bad crawling towards our door. Terry sometimes goes in with him at the weekend but Dad told him not to bother, there was hardly any business. Greg, the guy Dad had with him, has left for the States. I'm glad for Greg, he's a physics graduate who just couldn't get a job, so, rather than do nothing he worked for a pittance at the bikeshop. It was so peculiar, Dad and he really got on, true mates, almost like father and son. Dad in work is a different person, it's as if he sheds a miserable cloak and puts on a smile as soon as he unlocks the shop door. I know it's not the job, it's the customers, and it was Greg.

I tried to find out a bit more regarding Ms. Wolfe and himself.

'That stuck-up woman. We were at school together, the same year.'

She looks about ten years younger; that's what money does for you.

'But she always had her cap set on a doctor. Went to all the nurses' dances when she was in college. No teacher for her, a medical man, nothing less. She got her man all right. Poor old Niall. Talk about being snared.'

Mum looked up from scanning the crossword with a 'do not say anything more' expression on her face.

'Who's scared?' Jenny wanted to know. She was staggering around trying to get her trousers off. Dave had just informed her that the paddling pool was filled and that Fernando was drinking all the water.

No more information on the Wolfe front. But I sense scandal. Mum asked me to take Fernando and Terry for a walk. I don't think she saw the pathetic connection between the two. Belle and Shazz were plastered in baby lotion, out to catch the rays. Dave, not complaining, had been roped in to mow the grass. Normally he moans. I'm sure some of his past protests are still being processed in the White House. But today, nothing. Please notice that he's trying, please Mum and Dad.

As we walked through the Park we were saluted by all the new neighbours. Strange. For what feels like miles there are bungalows, two-storey houses like ours, and there's a mansion affair being constructed right at the entrance. We even have a shop now, run by Mr. and Mrs. Eglinton. He used to be a solicitor in Gloucestershire but lost most of his money when Lloyd's crashed. I don't understand what it was all about but, with debts paid off, their children grown and flown, they decided to move to France. Apparently they trotted off to the Dordogne and found just the place they wanted. Then their daughter got divorced and had nowhere to live; she refused to live in France. I would have left her in the middle of the mess. How dare she make them change their plans. However, they took her and her two little boys for a short holiday in West Cork to get over her broken marriage. When, lo and behold, they heard about the planning permission for a small general store with accommodation, a house to be exact. And that's how they ended up here. Dad thinks it's disgusting, all these foreigners wandering in and buying property. He says it's a takeover. I tried to point out that I fully intend to live in England, America, Africa, everywhere. So, he might as well get used to the fact that other people are going to be doing the same.

Terry and I walked the poor dog until his feet were ready to fall off. A weary Fernando is good for the family. We eventually let him off the lead to chase whatever he thought he could see down by the river. It seemed as if everyone we know was out and swimming. Mum won't let us near the water, says there are rats in it. Apparently, according to Margaret, we'll all get Weil's disease. How come all my friends aren't dropping like flies, and how come someone like Margaret knows so much about medical things? She probably doesn't use a pillow, she goes to sleep on a First Aid manual. According to Dora, who lives at least three miles away but knows absolutely everything about everybody, Margaret and Kerry are having problems. That's the way Dora talks. Kerry has been coming home late and is often seen in hotels, in bars, etc., etc. Mum, who likes everything to be neat and rosy, said that he was doing business no doubt. Dora replied, but what kind of business? I'd lost interest at that point so left them to figure it all out. But, there is a point to this: I don't want to lose my baby-sitting cash.

Donie joined us for the walk back. Donie is about six foot five, extremely good looking and knows it. Sometimes he's all right but he tends to sneer at everything you say. He's got this smart mother, smart as in attractive and pleasant, his dad's one of the founder members of the golf club and decidedly wealthy. Money again. He's not all bad I suppose. By the time we got back and Terry and Donie had disappeared upstairs to check over maths problems, Mum needed me to take Jenny out because she was trying to prepare a special dinner for Dad. Why does she bother?

'Mother. I have exams. On Monday.' It's true, scarily true.

'Please don't argue.' Her voice was tired, she looked crumpled. Mum can do that, look as if she hasn't slept for a week and she's just had bad news from the bank manager, all rolled into one.

43

'And please will you ring Granny when you get back. One of the nurses said that she's been anxious to talk to you.'

Why doesn't Mum talk to her, I want to know? Poor old Granny Luckmore, she really is ancient. She lives in an old peoples' home about twenty miles away. She used to be in Dublin but Dad hated the drive, we hated the drive, and the new place is cheaper. Sometimes when we visit she almost sounds normal. The last time that we went to see her it was as if she was disappearing in front of our eyes. The collar of her blouse was so big, it looked as if she was going to be swallowed up. She smokes like a chimney, her little claw hands grasping the cigarette as if that's the only thing that keeps her going. It probably is. But her mouth! Between the false teeth and the millions of little lines, I tell you, it's enough to guarantee that I will not smoke. Dora and Dave watch out. Occasionally Mum smokes. She looks stupid, not a natural. Dora has a face like an underfed skeleton at the best of times, so I ignore her.

Jen and I, plus dog, set off towards the village this time. It isn't a village any more. Ireland is expanding. Thank you Europe!!! We're on the road to Killarney, so lots of traffic passes through. There's talk of a cyber café. That I don't think will happen. Baltinogar has only recently got used to the idea of electricity. I saw the woman with the satellite dish bird table coming out of the greengrocer's. She waved, I waved, Jen waved and Fernando lifted his leg against the pushchair. He is so disgusting. But the sun was shining and everyone seemed in lovely humour.

I should be learning about the liver fluke, memorising *King Lear*. Great! Dad and Mum are downstairs finishing off their dinner and they seemed fairly OK. No they didn't. That's what I want it to be like. Dad looks, how does he look? Burnt out, derelict, empty. What are we going to do with Granny Luckmore? Is she going to have to live with us, because, according to Dad, there's no way that we can afford to pay for her anymore? I'm going to be honest with you, book, I promised I would. Granny L would be better off dead. And now I wish I hadn't thought it or written it. But by the time I rang her and one of the helpers passed the receiver to her she didn't even know who I was. She kept saying 'Anna who?' Don't ask me, I felt like replying. I haven't the remotest idea either. See you tomorrow, book.

◉ *Nine*

I can't even cry. Fernando was knocked down this afternoon, before we got back from school. No tears. No more Fernando.

Belle's snoring. If only I had my own room. Dad used to talk about converting the loft. I'm not going to mention how I feel because I feel too much.

Soft nose snuffling.

Friend.

Foolish hound.

Finished.

Sentimental crap. But it's how I feel. Do you feel like this tonight, birth mother? I haven't mentioned you for a while and not at all here in this new journal. Are you a stupid sentimentalist? I'm never, never going to own a pet. I hate Kerry McCarthy. Mum said he tore into the

Park at about forty miles an hour, she keeps saying thank God it wasn't a child. He didn't even apologise, just left him there for Mum to carry in. How could he? No more 'feckees'.

Ten

Wednesday 9th . . . 10 pm . . . Four more exams to go. Dave has a fortnight to revise. He disappeared straight after tea and hasn't been seen since; not even for the dog's burial. Granny Luckmore used to say, out of sorrow comes forth sweetness. I didn't understand that remark until something strange happened.

I've just met the two most extraordinary people. They're the weirdos who recently moved in, but they're not weird at all, they're fantastic. His name is Christian, he's Dutch, and her name is Maud, she's Irish but speaks with a terribly, terribly smart accent. He used to make documentaries. Terry and he really got on. Terry is going to be something exceptional in the future. I know it. I only wish that he did. Dad will have to take everything back. This evening Dad did his old trick. He puts on this tired, bored kind of voice.

'Come on now, son.'

When does he ever say 'son'? OK, he did then, but it was not normal.

'Give Christian and Maud a break.'

You could tell that Christian was enjoying talking about cameras and all the new technology.

'Call round, tomorrow if you like. I'll show you some of the equipment.' You could tell that Mr. Anderrsun was embarrassed by Dad. If I were Mum I'd tell him to shut up.

They were invited round for a drink. Mum's been going to home wine-making classes. Some of it is really strong. Terry and I kind of borrowed a bottle the night we got our Junior Cert results. Poor old Mum thought that we'd got some unknown disease. I didn't have the heart to tell her that we had a multiple hangover. She's heavily into social studies, goes to this adult learning thingy, and brings her new-found knowledge into everything we say and do. If she so much as caught a whiff of one of the many cigarettes that I know Dave smokes, she'd have him straight into drug rehab. According to one of her many new theories, those who smoke definitely end up putting something else with their tobacco. How come she doesn't apply that rule to Dora?

Maud's a naturalist. Yes, I thought the same at first; visions of the pair of them floating round their bird table in the nude. But no. She writes for magazines all over the world. I've read some of her stuff in newspapers. Her particular favourites are . . . yes, rooks. I thought they were all crows, but no, the dirty dive-bombers are rooks. Anyway, she saw the Fernando accident. That's how she and

49

Mum got talking. She asked me how I felt. I couldn't answer. Then she said something extraordinary.

'I think it's very presumptuous of us to believe that we are the only ones entitled to an afterlife.'

If Father Casimir heard that, he'd have her in prison.

'What about cows and sheep?' I wanted to know. The abattoir isn't exactly an animal version of The Hilton.

'I don't eat meat. Haven't for years. None of the children have. In fact, when we had household pets they didn't either. Except for the cat of course, the perfect meat-eating monster.'

This got me very confused.

'We can choose; animals can't.' There'd have been no point in telling my departed friend that the chicken carcasses he devoured weren't the best treat for a canine. He didn't even seem to mind choking on the small bones. It wasn't until I watched a children's programme with Jen that I discovered you weren't meant to give dogs treats like that. Ah well!

Maud mulled the choice idea over for a while.

'But once they give themselves over to us as pets then we do the choosing for them.'

Strange lady!

'Have you ever read *The Little Prince*?'

I haven't, I must check if it's in the library.

'I'm sure your Fernando enjoyed his rabbits on the run, but we also know for certain that the rabbit didn't enjoy the running.'

All right, so . . . she's still a bit weird but I could listen to her for hours. She's a bit like Sally. I must introduce
them, once Sally's better. She's refused to go and have her
back operated on; she goes to all kinds of alternative
experts. I think it's madness, so does Amy.

'I believe we can either choose to mimic that part of
God's world which is cruel and predatory, mirror the terrible in His universe with our sophisticated weapons,
parade our dark souls . . .'

This woman can talk and talk. Dad was shifting about.

'More wine, Maud?'

'Yes please, Robert. It's gone straight to my toes.'

Dad flashed her a look that suggested he would rather
like it to go to her brain and put her to sleep.

'Where was I?'

'Predators, mirrors, weak and strong.' Terry had been
absorbing everything. Belle had disappeared ages ago, I
could hear her spicing things up in the bedroom.

'Oh yes. I don't believe that it is all some shocking game.
I believe that we are given the intellect to make choices.'

WOW!

Mum really likes her. Good, that might throw Dora
off the scent. The last thing Maud said was to never forget the joy or the pain of anything. And then she said the
best thing of all.

'Write it all down. Then it's there, forever, well, as long
as you or someone you've invited wants to read it. Where
would we be without all those Egyptian hieroglyphics?'

God, she's brilliant. Thank you.

⟳ Eleven

Thursday 10th May . . . almost ten o'clock. It looks
beautiful outside, semi-bright and perfect. I am beginning
to believe that I should never have written the entry on
Sunday about something dark happening. Because it's as
if I've opened the door to hell.

There was a big row tonight. By big I mean enor-
mously huge. Terry wouldn't eat his beef. It was so simple; badly-timed but simple. He apologised, said that he
loved Mum's cooking, but, he was making a choice. Dad
went into orbit.

'Do you think that I work in that bicycle shop six
days a week to bring home the money to pay for good
food to have you refuse it?'

Dad didn't draw a breath.

'Sorry, Dad. I appreciate it.'

Terry actually replied. Dave had his fork poised ready to take the meat from Terry's plate. Mum and Jen, who was sitting on Mum's lap, kind of chewed in harmony. Jen's got a cold. Maud suggested all kinds of natural remedies, has left a little collection of coloured herbal medicines on the work surface, which I know Dad could see from where he was sitting, glaring bulgingly at Terry. Maud and Sally are emphatically on the same wavelength. Dad doesn't have an enormous amount of time for Sally either.

'Get out! Get away from the table. Go and eat with your new friends, the Anderrsuns. Load of New Age claptrap.'

Jenny liked claptrap and began to sing cheerily to the tune of Three Blind Mice.

'Clap clap trap.'

There's no stopping the musical genius once she gets going. I can still hear her singing in her bed, only it's become 'clop trop' over the last few minutes.

Terry's home. Frag came and collected him and Dave in his Mum's car. He's already seventeen, so parades around by bringing himself to school. I went out with him once, but, without too much sacrifice, decided that Terry needed a good friend far more than I needed a boyfriend. They called over to Donie's and one or two others who hang round together. According to Terry they got quite a bit of work done, even Dave. I didn't, I can't. I feel tight and panicky. Luckily Dad didn't bump into either of them; I could definitely smell beer. Terry asked me if I thought he was right about the not eating

53

meat thing. If he thinks it's right, I suppose it is for him. To be perfectly honest I've been contemplating forgoing meat. Some of those tragic pictures in the newspapers of young people dying with BSE or whatever, CJD. Well, it all seems a bit of a sacrifice that two creatures have to die. As opposed to that, I love Mum's roasts. The potatoes all soaked and golden. And what about Christmas? No turkey? I mean, turkeys aren't exactly the brightest of things. I'll have to have a think.

The phone's ringing. Dad's yelling at me to get downstairs before I wake up the house . . . Logical?!!!

11.10 pm. Maybe the dark clouds are rolling away. I'm smiling as I write. Bliss, double treble bliss. Amy just rang, Andrew's coming home. Apparently Sally was doing a jig; she really misses him, she forgot all about her back. Maybe she was right about letting things heal on their own. Ollie, the dad, he's a sweetie, he's a kind of plumber handyman. I must tell Maud and Christian about him, just in case they need work doing. My tiny version of networking. As well as Amy and Andrew there's Paul and Colm and Seb. Amy's the youngest. Sometimes she gets really hacked off with the boys' teasing, so she legs it over here. She and Terry are almost like boyfriend and girl-friend, except Terry's too backward to ask her out, plus he's convinced himself that he's ugly. I don't even know if she fancies him. It's kind of a taboo subject. She knows that I like Andrew, but it really is the only big secret between us. I couldn't expose that. Does Dave know? I don't think so. When I caught him thumbing through the tissue pages of my first diary, he was right at the end. Probably looking for ammunition from the night before. I wish Mum wouldn't keep saying that everything's to do with his age. I was once his age and I wouldn't have dreamt of reading someone else's letters or diaries. I give up.

Dave's got really bad tonsillitis. He's wrapped in a sleeping bag now, despite the temperature reaching Sahara strength. The doctor says he needs his tonsils out. Dad says he needs to sleep and study; Dave that is, not Dad.

Still no news about Jacob and Tina. I re-read it the other night. I have a horrible sinking feeling that it's a complete loser. All that work. All those late nights. How do writers put up with rejection? I think I'll die or something if it's sent back. Some of the things published I've read haven't been that great. I don't want Ruth to be right. Everything is always so hunky-happy for her. She says that it isn't, that she gets lonely at home, that her mum is always out, that she longs for a big family, a baby sister or brother. But I've seen the look on her face when we're clearing up at teatime, or emptying the linen basket, or doing the lawn-mowing rota. She looks relieved when her mother pulls up in her four-wheel drive. And that's another mystery. How come they, with one child, end up with a gigantic people-carrier type vehicle, while we have to stuff ourselves into Dad's ancient car. Four in the back, JM on Mum's knee, Dad muttering obscenities about slow drivers. He reckons that they're all women picking their children up from school. Even when the person behind the wheel is patently male, he refers to them disparagingly as she. Is it any wonder that he's producing rejects for sons?

Now I can hear fighting downstairs. I shake inside when this happens, knowing they're down there, arguing. Mum doesn't even argue; she suggests, then gets verbally battered with Dad's drone. I sometimes think we'd all be better off if they divorced. I know that Mum tries to keep the peace. But what's the point? I suppose Dad just doesn't respect her anymore. She always gives in, always apologises first. I've watched enough Oprah and Kilroy to know that people can have different opinions. I'm never getting married, I look at the pair of them and I know that I couldn't endure the bitterness. They've been together for eighteen years. A murderer, a rapist, a child abuser is back on the streets ready to carry on after ten or twelve. No. I don't understand.

It's well after midnight. Get used to failure, Anna; no study done. Mum and I have just shared a cup of tea. She'd been crying and all round her eyes are tiny lines which stay there. I asked her.

'Is it worth it?'

She didn't say anything.

'You could work, get a job and a life to go with it. Dad doesn't deserve you.'

Then she sobbed out all her guilt about being a bad wife, a bad mother, a bad person.

'I can't be disloyal.'

Why?

'He's my husband.'

So?

'Sometimes I wish I had a friend,' she cried.

Jesus.

I hugged her. She's probably the loneliest person I know living in a house with six others.

Twelve

Friday 11th May . . . In the kitchen. Dave's too sick to care and Mum and Dad are talking quietly in the TV room. Terry's trying to repair Jen's talking book and Belle is at Shazza's.

I've blown it, everything. Gone to pieces. I am nuclear fallout. Amy and I have had the biggest fight. How? Easy. How the hell did I know that Andrew was coming home with a fiancée? The last time he brought a girlfriend home was a disaster. Her name was Fleur and she was pathetic. This one's called Olivia.

'Daddy's Irish, Mummy's French, so I suppose I'm Frirish!'

That was a joke? They all laughed. Amy had shown her all her music collection, her paintings; she's really good at art. Sally and Ollie were digging around in drawers to display old family photographs, Seb and Colm and Paul were falling over themselves making her coffee.

'No. I love instant.'

I'd love to instantly obliterate her. I mean, for heaven's sake. Who is she?

'Well, my lovely Anna. What do you think?'

Andrew and I were in the kitchen. I wanted to tell him about my book, Mum, poor Fernando. Fernando really liked him, used to go berserk when the clapped-out old car arrived. Sorry Fernando. Your taste in people was almost as bad as your taste in edibles. Fernando could empty a dustbin before you said RUBBISH. The lot – tissues, potato peelings, laddered tights. UUGGHHHH! I miss your huge head resting on my knee when I read.

Andrew actually asked me what I thought of Olivia.

'She's nice,' I lied. I lie all the time. I think I don't but you, my friendly diary, you know differently. I lie when Dad says, 'Is all your homework done?' When Mum looks at me with those quizzical droopy eyes, 'You're sure you're all right?' My stomach's in knots, my head's done an extra Exorcist turn, my hands are clammy and my feet are cold. But of course I'm fine. Not being fine would mean that she'd have to pay eighteen pounds for me to go to the doctor. Which Mum had to do again this afternoon with Dave. He's had a blood test, he's probably got glandular fever. And now my jaw's aching. It's my wisdom teeth but. . . No, I'm grand. I lie again and again.

'Honestly, Anna, you're going to love her.'

Just like Fleur, the sociologist. I don't think so.

'Her mum's amazing.'

Marry the mother. Once she gets osteoporosis you can be all mine.

'She's a community midwife in Cambridge.'

WOW! Imagine!!!

'She works days at a time.'

I've already given you permission to marry her.

'They're so proud. Olivia's being a doctor and everything.'

He was bashing around in the fridge, finding butter and ham and lettuce.

'Do you want a sandwich?'

I shook my head. And then informed him I was going to ring Dad to collect me. Yeah, I know, danger; asking Dad to do anything but repair bicycles is a pretty risky business. But it was Mum's nightclass. She walks; he doesn't even offer her a lift. Pig.

Amy was really concerned.

'Have you got a migraine?'

Recently that's been another regular event. Suddenly it's like I'm in a corridor, my nose and the side of my face feels. . . it's not just my nose and the side of my face, everything's on red alert. Then, magic moment, smells change and a jagged knife dives behind my left eye. The rest is boring because it involves being sick, not being able to think the right words, numb hands and finally a God-awful headache that lasts for a day and a night. Belle always manages to have to do some recording as I'm lying there, in darkness. Forget peace; peace and the Fieldings didn't quite arrive as a package.

I'm going grey with embarrassment.

'What does he see in her?'

Why, oh why did I say that?

'Sorry?'

Amy's little and fair, both fair-headed and straight. She knew, I knew, that neither of us know Olivia. I could only see Andrew's hand on Olivia's knee, her lovely moulded, rounded knee. Mine stick out like lumps in a mattress. Hers are curves. Mother, birth mother, was he a giant? Was my father some stick insect you felt sorry for? Olivia's mother was, is, a princess, and Andrew's going to marry her.

'Well, I mean, marrying her. He's only twenty-two. What does he want to go and get married for?'

Amy sat down.

'Twenty-three, and sometimes Anna you can be a real mystery. You take on no-hopers like Donie, Frag, Razor.'

History . . . history.

'She's perfect. She's bright, she's lovely, she's really good for Andy.'

'Is that me you're talking about?'

He'd come in for more beer. He drinks too much. She's turning him into an alcoholic. She's five years older than he is. That feels wrong.

'Well?'

I tried to explain to Amy that I didn't mean it the way it sounded. She called me a bigot. That wasn't it, any of it. She told me I ought to get my head out of romance novels and back into the real world. Me? Then she said what really hurt.

'Grow up, Anna. According to Mum, your book is so childish she couldn't believe that you'd sent it off.'

Betrayal. Sally, Andrew, then Amy. I don't honestly want to wake up tomorrow. Please fast-forward my life, God. Get me to a good bit.

Twelve

Monday May 14th . . . French. What more can I say about Ms. Wolfe than that she told the whole class we were useless. Thank you, Ms. Wolfe. That's guaranteed to send us scuttling to *Le Figaro*, or whatever their lousy French newspaper's called, which I've insisted that Mum orders from Mr. Eglinton even though it costs way too much. I'm sixteen and I know that if you keep telling someone they're bad, dumb, useless, or, in my case, in need of a lot more attention to gender detail, you end up frightened of even more failure. I went back to entry 1 a few moments ago: Tuesday April 17th. Scary how things can change. Well, this is going to be my second 12th entry, no number 13 is going to shower even more misfortune on my red head! Shouldn't a good biblical number work in my favour? 12 disciples and all that? Am

I the only person in the whole world who thinks strange connections, odd ideas? Maybe I am mad and Dora is right. Maybe I shouldn't exist. But I do. And now is the moment I've been waiting for. Time to turn you upside down, my copy, my friend. You, diary. I can write on the other side. Here goes. I'm not being superstitious, I'm still trying to be positive. Please let everything turn round with me.

Here I am . . . 10 pm . . . Belle's been allowed to see the end of 'Pride and Prejudice', I'll explain why in a moment. Bad news needs keeping. (Well away from me would be good. But.)

I went over to see Maud after school. Her place is full of wooden masks, blue glass, vases of flowers and books, so many books in boxes, on shelves, overflowing onto the floor. No carpets, bare wooden blocks, already scraped from stuff being dragged over them. The furniture is huge, two giant settees puffed up and waiting for someone to flop into them. They look as if they'd eat you, they're so big and squashy. Just one table; it looms as long as one of the giant settees, but it can't be, their house isn't that much bigger than ours, although I suppose it has to be. Maybe not; ours is overflowing with us, theirs is overflowing with everything they've gathered. Amazing. Maud, half specs perched on the end of her nose, asked me if everything was all right. Why did she do that? Couldn't she see it in my eyes, that I haven't slept, that I've been given another dumb project, that my body opted out of menstruation and went for full-flood instead? I don't know. Then she apologised.

'Tell me if you want to. When you're ready. Carrot cake?' she offered.

I was studying the kitchen. There are jars and jars of beans and rice, all shades, a pasta-making machine – I know that's what it is because I asked – an olive oil container that could fill our tank in the garden; well, not quite, but this bottle would take Hercules to tip. Coffee was brewed, cake was served. I ate it. It was nice enough, not as good as Sally's.

Amy didn't talk to me at all today. She's never done that before. I can't bear it. Ruth was away. Ruth is always away. I don't know why her parents bother sending her to school at all. If she doesn't have flu she has asthma, if she doesn't have asthma she has eczema, if that fails she's suffering from nervous exhaustion. But I know exactly where she is, she's in Dublin going to a charity fashion show. She'll be rubbing shoulders with Bono and his missus, Sylvester Stallone and all the beautiful people from planet filmland. Ruth probably sees Amy and me as charity cases, in need of support from a rich friend. No, she just sees me like that.

Maud took me up to one of the bedrooms. It smelt strange. I can't describe what it was like, dry, bone dry, a bit like a graveyard.

'Meet Beaky.'

She pulled back a blanket and revealed a large cage, inside which was a huge baby bird. I know huge and baby don't go together, but think elephant. Got the picture? The poor thing was mostly bald, with little blood streaks down its fluffy wing bit. I sympathised.

'Cat got it,' Maud explained.

'Clever cat. We ought to send it up K2, Everest, Mont Blanc.' The trees round this place are not tall, they're enormous. That's probably why Dad elected to drop us here, make me feel at home with the giant greenery.

'No, silly. He fell, or most probably was pushed.'

Oh God, nature's freaks are everywhere in Baltinogar.

'Why would a bird family do that?'

This was a more personal question than she knew. I haven't told her yet about being adopted. Maybe Mum has. It's not that it's a secret, but I always feel I'd rather be the one to do the explaining. Mum makes me feel like something out of a Disney cartoon.

'And then we saw you.'

Remind you of Dumbo?

'With your coppery curls.'

She still can't bring herself to call them red. Occasionally she does, blushes like mad and reverts to copper or gold.

Maud was busily putting the blanket back over the cage. The bird's eyes were glazed shut, a tiny shadow of skin across the bulge.

'Maybe he's diseased, maybe they had a successful clutch and he's the weakest. Who knows.'

'Will he die?' Fair question. Death seems to have taken up residence here lately.

'Might do. But at least I can keep a close eye on him here. No cats.'

I like cats. So does Maud. But, as she said, better not to have too many around while she's doing her home-nursing course with Beaky. And what a beak. It looks like it could scythe your fingers in a snap. And this is a baby!

Downstairs Christian was bashing away on his word processor. He's writing a book about a trip that he made to the Amazon. Imagine! The Amazon. My father has never been out of this country; my mother has, once, to London. Once. I've never been on a plane or a boat. I have been on a train, when we went to see *King Lear*. It really felt like living.

'Tell Terry that I have some new packages for him,' Christian announced, absent-mindedly feeling round his desk for his glasses. Maud pushed them from the top of his head onto his nose. They still love each other. I felt jealous.

The packages sounded exciting. I like getting presents. I'd like even more to get a letter about my book.

'There's one here that Barry sent.'

I looked quizzical.

'Grandson Barry. Did Maud tell you that he and Tyler are coming over next weekend?'

'This weekend, Chris.'

Maud was breezing around the room picking up discarded papers, pencils with their ends completely chewed away. There's a kind of easy contentment about the two of them.

Maybe if Dad had travelled, Mum got a job?

'Who are Barry and Tyler?' Odd names. I can't think I'm too keen on their names, whoever they are.

'The grandsons. Barry's sixteen . . .'

'Seventeen, darling, and Tyler's eighteen. They both managed to get chicken-pox after Christmas so, instead of doing their 'A' Levels their parents took them to the States for a while, and then on to Greece.'

Who are these exotic people who do things out of the ordinary? I'm sure that's the kind of family I was meant to join. Their parents are Billie and Henry. No, not two guys in a get-together; Billie is Maud and Christian's daughter, Henry's the dad. Henry writes music and Billie does more or less what her parents did. Oh, God help me, that means, if I follow in my lots' footsteps, I'll either be a hassled mother or a harried father/bicycle mender. I want out.

I thought things couldn't get worse. They can. Dad's shop is being closed down definitely. O'Conor maintains that he over-extended himself with his restaurants and video shops. He's consolidating. Well, if consolidating is Dad downstairs drinking Mum's extra strong wine and crying, that's quite some extension. I'm frightened; even Belle and Dave are quiet. In fairness, Dave's throat is so sore he can't move. We don't have any money. I'm really scared. Will we end up like some of the kids at school, the very poor, the genuinely poor? I don't think I've known what poor is until this moment. Dave, in a flash of contrite panic, whispered he'd give up smoking. He didn't think that Dad was listening; suddenly Dad just broke down. We've broken our parents.

Second 12th entry ... I don't care about 'The Jacob Dream'. The only thing I care about is tomorrow; not anything more exciting than a better tomorrow, an ordinary, everyday tomorrow. Please.

✺ Fourteen

Don't forget, 13 does not exist. Maybe skipping the unluckiest number in the world will shift everything back into place. Am I insane? Probably. As I was getting off the bus this morning I saw something incredible: two young people, a boy and a girl, older than me but not by much. He was in a wheelchair and she was on crutches – but very small, not full height. She was bending down towards him and they were about to kiss. They looked perfect, in every way. And I thought these words.

> Two beautiful broken bodies
> Joined in a triangle
> Circling defeat.

It felt like a prayer. I tried to carry it back with me because the situation at home isn't strained, it's gone beyond that. I can still see them, somewhere behind my eyes. But now it makes me want to weep, not celebrate.

According to Mum, Dad's received some sort of compensation, enough for him to take two or three months off, finish the garden, decorate the bedrooms in readiness for us to sell the place. Why? Because houses in this area are suddenly sought after. Wouldn't you know it? Just as we become socially acceptable, we're taking off again into the unacceptable bracket. I'm not a snob, but is it so wrong to want to be comfortable?

I don't like to ask too many questions, which means that I've got a permanent headache from keeping quiet. Every time I think I might have a reasonable conversation with Mum, Dad walks in all sweaty, it's hot outside, or thirsty, same reason. He's looking really ill. Not shouting, not talking, but he is drinking a lot.

'Why don't you get rid of that last batch?' I asked Mum. It's the remains of a five-gallon container of peach and apple. I wouldn't dare try it. According to Mum it's not very strong, but seeing as she only drinks by the liqueur-glass-full and Dad by the pint, how does she know? Terry and I are accidentally going to knock it over tonight. We're scheming to get Jenny-M involved; that way we might get away with it.

Terry's been recording music for Dave all afternoon. I wish Mum would do something about Dave, he's really sick. All his glands are swollen, he can hardly swallow, he can't talk. We're disintegrating.

The pathetic thing about all this renovation is that Dad's useless at it. Cupboards he puts up fall down. He laid stair carpet and forgot to fasten the treads; Mum wan-

71

dered round in an elastic bandage for days looking like old Mother Hubbard. I tried to persuade her to wear trousers to hide the ugly, wrinkly stocking effect.

'I couldn't, pet I'm too plump.'

No worry that she'll get any plumper; we've had baked beans and soup three times this week. Mum's making brown bread and Sky's gone. I miss the extra channels, I miss Sky News, even if it is depressing. I miss Sky Movies. Most of all I miss Amy. She's in Galway. No phone call, no message, no anything. The whole family has gone up to see Sally's family, to introduce them to Olivia.

Now I must wait, till Dave and Belle are asleep. Jen's in her own little bed that Dad has stuck into the tiny room that goes over the stairs. If it's six foot by four foot that's an exaggeration. I'd feel like a prisoner in a cell, like Oscar. My beloved Oscar Wilde. Why wasn't I alive a hundred years ago? I don't know. He, Keats and me, some island, loads of paper and a pen or three. Mind you, then I really would feel out of touch. I don't only miss television, I REALLY MISS AMY.

✺ Fifteen

It's break time. Terry knows about the new diary. We're sitting under a tree, on our own. Frag's having to clear up the canteen with Donie because they were caught going to the shop yesterday. Pathetic. Rules are fine but make them worth something. Suddenly Mr. Kennedy has gone power crazy. Dave's still got tonsillitis or whatever. His Junior Cert is almost happening and he and Mum are going to the doctor again. Poor Mum actually pleaded with Dad. We're going to have to apply for medical cards. So what? If we haven't got money to pay, we haven't got money to pay. I suggested contacting Sean. Mum looked up hopefully. Dad walked out of the kitchen and kicked the back door shut.

Belle's on her school trip. She started packing at six o'clock. One hair brush, one make-up bag. If I went on, there'd be no room left to cover the real story. Belle is totally unaffected by last night.

Last night was another BIG mistake, not small. The family seems to be indulging in an excess of horror. When we got downstairs to drain the contents of the five-gallon drum, Dad was asleep, head on the table. Dad was drunk. I've never seen him drunk. I've seen him angry, sad, occasionally happy. He was snoring and the whole kitchen was full of a sickly sweet smell, fermenting fruit. Oh, Mum! What a stupid hobby! It was all right when he had a job.

But now. It's all Sally's fault. She and Mum got really close after Terry got into huge trouble at school. It was a long time ago, but he was into some pretty scary company and ended up in a police cell. Sally was really supportive, and, because Mum was all flushed with new friends (it's too long a story – if anyone else is reading this you'll have to go back to the loft diary), she took up all sorts of new stuff. Hence the wine-making.

Back to Dad, who was ranting and raving like a madman last night. I tucked Jen in beside me because Mum asked me to. Belle actually cried herself to sleep. Does she remember? Nope. All I could hear was silence from Dave's and Terry's room. Dad hit Terry. He's never, never hit any of us. Mum kept saying that Dad didn't mean it. I don't care. He did it. He shouldn't. What went wrong was Jen. She was half-dopey asleep; this was obviously not one of her creature of the night sessions. We were carrying the container to the sink when Jen decided that she'd sit on Dad's knee. The idea was that we'd say that Jen had wandered out of her bed, gone downstairs, looking for the dog seemed like a good excuse. She's a pretty thick kid, forgetting that her Nando was dead was a working possibility. Then the plan should have been that Terry heard her, I heard Terry, and that, somehow, in the dark, she'd managed to take the lid off the five gallons and was attempting to drink it. Looking back it was pretty hopeless as a plan.

At the time it felt plausible, until the lap-climbing incident. Dad woke with a start just as Terry and I were trying to unseal the damned wine.

I won't repeat what Dad said, or what he said to Mum. This is it. The family is now in tiny violent pieces. Nothing will ever be the same again. All this sunshine and I don't know if I can last another night.

✺ Sixteen

Thank you, thankyou God. It's Friday the eighteenth of May and the house is empty. Jen's over at Maud's. They seem to get on famously. Poor old Beaky (still with us, getting noisier) had better watch out. He hasn't seen what Jen can do to a Barbie doll. Dave is a bit better, so he's been allowed to watch television with his new friends up the road. I used to dream of boys moving in here, interesting, handsome, mysterious boys. But they're all either babies or sub-human. So much for dreams. Still, Maud's grandsons are arriving tomorrow. Who knows!! Belle and Shazza are being taken to the ballet with Dora and Tom. Poor old Toby – since he and Dave fell out, he'll probably have to go too.

'It's good for them, Veronica.'

That's what Dora calls Mum. Nickie is what Dad calls

her when he's in a good mood, which was probably about the time that Moses came down the mountain with the Ten Commandments.

'Ballet broadens horizons.'

If you say so, Dora. I like the music, but I don't like hearing feet scraping around the stage. We went last term to see *Swan Lake*. I couldn't believe it; some of the cygnets looked as if they'd escaped from Granny L's nursing home.

Mum has taken Dad to see Father Casimir. Why not Matt again? Mum shushed me and explained that they both felt a little embarrassed that, after all the help they'd had in the past, they were now back to square one. I wish we lived in New York. Then there'd be so many people with problems, nobody would bother with us. Dad looked grey and blotchy this morning. He's apologised to Terry again and again. Terry has told him it's all right. The bruise on his left cheek says it's all wrong, but Terry refuses to bear grudges. Dave's bottom lip is permanently stuck out like a mean I'm-about-to-bite bull terrier. I know that Terry won't retaliate. Beware of Dave. Dad; he will. He's not afraid of anything.

School was. That's it. End-of-term exams are over. I think I've failed the lot. I don't care. I'm thinking really seriously of getting a job in a hotel or somewhere. At least then I'd have a roof over my head, food sometimes and I'd be away from all this. This is much worse than anything that's ever happened. Ms. Spillane has told me to wait. What for? She's recently got engaged to Matt the psychol-

77

ogist, our family therapist over all the trouble that Terry found himself in. I don't know what Ms. Spillane sees in Matt. He's not even good-looking. I don't know why she wants to get married. Why's everybody getting married? Andrew? Where are you? He hasn't even called up, even though I know he'd like to see Terry and Mum. If he'd been around over the last few days, maybe things would be different. It's all down to Sally. She's the most treacherous person I know. To say something about my book to Amy and not to me. That's such a breach of trust. She's always preaching about honesty. Well, so much for her version of honesty. I reckon that she's the biggest hypocrite out.

I couldn't tell Ms. Spillane everything. You can't talk openly about your family. That would be like giving in, relinquishing control. I don't know – it's that frightening thought that we're spiralling away from one another. I hate O'Conor, the bikeshop owner. He was an opportunist who bought Dad out in the first place. It's not that Dad is like Ollie. Ollie used to be a bank manager and then ditched it for what he calls his real job. Ollie has a brand new van, three young guys working with him, and is paying to support two sons in England – well, one now that Andrew's trained and engaged and about to be married. Hold on, the doorbell is about to drop off. I miss you, Fernando, I miss your stupid barking.

It's after six and I'm crying. Why am I crying? Because I've just read the last entry about Fernando. I can't stand this dwelling, this sugary luxury of soaking in pain. It's not how I want to be. I bet my father, my sperm-dad, does this, sobs occasionally about the beautiful woman he left to go to sea, to the dentist, back to his mother. I'm boiling with rage about Kerry McCarthy. First of all that was him at the door. All happy chuckly 'baby-sit tonight?' No full sentence, just suntan and cheese smile. He's got amazing teeth. They're probably painted. Nobody's teeth are that white. Mine aren't.

'No.'

I know, book, I know. Manners maketh man. Grandmother Luckmore used to say those kind of things to me. Do unto others as you'd have them do unto you. OK, Granny L. I'll go round, chuck whatever his favourite thing is on the road, then run it over. He didn't mention the dog, not once.

'Are you sure, Anna?'

Weasly syrup wrapped round his smart voice, his big-shouldered suit blocking the door.

'We've got a bit of a thing going, tennis club dinner. Maggie's all dressed up. Disappointed. Y'know.'

Poor Adam, poor Chloe. Love thy neighbour as thyself.

'Do you believe that animals have a life after death?' Reasonable question. He stood his buckled-shoe ground, looked at the polish on his toe-tips, stuck his hands, plus signet ring on his baby finger, into his deep pockets.

'Never thought about it but, now that you ask, it's a nonsense. Obviously you aren't going to say yes. That's rather vindictive, young lady.'

Beware anyone who calls you young lady or young man. The two don't go together, youth and age. I could have called him bastard. But I didn't. I have dignity.

'The dog was out of control, on the road. Filthy thing. Margaret had already spoken to your parents about it.'

Parent. She'd never have talked to Dad like that; she's all cosy sweet and kind to Dad. All simper and curl.

'You killed a living thing, Mr. McCarthy. I honestly believe an apology would have made a difference.'

And he swung down the path, newly planted with pansies and marigolds, all in place for the first time ever because a set of big paws couldn't be given a chance to bury his latest bone, or one of Jen's dummies, or whatever crazy thing he'd nicked. He was a delinquent, and everywhere smells better, but nothing is better. He was hurt and wild and we tamed him and loved him and made him a bit more manic by chasing him, encouraging him. I'm so angry.

8.20 . . . Still angry. For the first time ever I want revenge. I think I'm going mad, despite having called round to Maud's and collected Jen, who is now practising being a lame rook. She's fluttering around the sitting room squawking. More later, I've just heard Dad and Mum arrive.

Not that it's ever going to happen, but if I ever become a bestseller it will be because I set up my writing desk in the bathroom. Here I am, almost midnight, locked in with all the lovely toilet smells. Yeutch . . . Belle's back, doing her dying swan act because Shazza wasn't allowed to stay. Of course she wasn't. Dear Dora has been informed of the latest Fielding trauma. Give Dora a whiff of scandal and she scuttles off like a road-runner. The whole world's turned Birdy!!!

Dad's going away. What good will that do? Dad's going to America – my parent who doesn't know the inside of an aeroplane from the inside of the only suit he's worn, his wedding suit. My Dad, the sixteen-year one, is going away. Can't write. Belle's dragging herself upstairs. Tomorrow's Saturday and Dad leaves at twelve.

◎ Seventeen

The fifth month, the nineteenth day, a weekend not like any other. No bikeshop, no bacon frying and toast dipped into the big yellow yolk puddle. No Dad. And it feels better.

I loved the airport. All sorts of goings on. Just in case this is in the future. I know that sounds big-headed, but even though I haven't heard a word from the publishers, surely that could be a good thing? I know, I know. I've been agonising about family and friends and disasters that are two-a-penny, but out there somewhere are Jacob and Tina. They're my invention.

Back to the airport. There's this statue of the hurler, Christy Ring. It's bronze and powerful. Imagine being able to make something like that? Then there's the pool with huge fish. Jen almost took a nose-dive, but Terry sat her on Jack Charlton's knee – that's another brilliant sculpture, Jack smiling, with his box of fishing stuff to one side. I felt so proud, all this is part of me. That's a fantastic feeling. Knowing that all these extras are a part of what makes you who you are. Mum took photographs after All Saints-spicy-Belle reminded her to take the cover off the lens. Mum was bright, is bright. Where did they get the money from? Why did they come back from Father Casimir's so perky? How come Father Casimir actually seems to have been able to get a result? Who knows? But I am glad Dad's gone. We all need a break from one another.

Terry's decided to get a job to help Mum out. Just up the road from us is a brand new garage. Terry asked Mum to drop him off on the way back from the airport. She thought he wanted sweets and said that she had a few left in the cupboard. I took a quick look at Dave, now in slow glandular recovery. He smirked. No, Mum, Dave's already absorbed the contents of the cupboard. Disgusting – I told you.

'No. I need something else,' Terry explained.

I honestly don't know what Mum thought he meant but she gave me a wink and drove into the forecourt. The guy who owns it was filling a car with petrol; he waved to Mum.

'Oh, it's Ted,' she said with a big smile. 'Ted,' window rolled down, an even bigger smile. I studied her as she chatted away. Bankruptcy, arguments, Dad gone – nothing showed in her face, just delight and pleasantries. It's an act. She's a full-blown actress.

'Please give my love to Eileen.'

We all exchanged looks. Eileen? Terry hopped out; he almost looked jaunty. For Terry to look jaunty takes a lot of courage. Over the years he's had a lot of problems. I suspect that I knew even when I was little that Terry and the outside world would never get on. I used to take the blame for everything, mud on the couch, towel chucked into the bath – he meant it to go on the side – all the milk drunk before breakfast. It didn't matter what the major crime was, it was always easier for me to be blamed. Dad doesn't so much treat us girls differently, it's more that he lays into the boys. Mum tries her hardest to be even-handed, but I know that I drive her 'round the bend' when I make snap judgements. Her problem is that she glows with love for everybody, honestly can't see that some people are genuinely rotten.

Take this Ted and Eileen. They were all at school together, because that's what Baltinogar is like. Once you're born here the chances of escape . . . unless you get out very young – Jenny-M really ought to be booking her ticket. Anyway, born here, marry here, die here seems to be the motto. Half the residents probably think the world is flat. They read the local paper, nothing wrong with that, but there is another life outside. There has to be, otherwise I am definitely giving up now, this minute. Back to Ted and Eileen. Mum and Eileen were once great friends, as close as Amy and I once were by the sound of it. Then she married Ted and they lived on his farm, then they lost a lot of money because of milk quotas and the

84

beef scare. Sad; according to Ted they were not doing badly, new farm machinery and so on. But my point is that Eileen could have contacted Mum, couldn't she? It always seems to be Mum who makes first moves. They've been exchanging Christmas cards for the last thousand years; in other words they knew our address. Whatever. They are calling round for tea tomorrow night. That means that the kitchen will be like an oven – baking, baking, and a bit more baking. But the smell of buns and apples and spices has to be one of the best in the world. I will have to take Jenny for one of her strolls so that Mum can have a couple of hours to herself. Dave will be missing. Hopefully Terry will be working. Mr. O'Sullivan (Ted to his mates) is thinking it over. Belle will be suffering for her beauty in front of the mirror; she'll either be plucking something or tie-dyeing her toe-nails. I have trouble looking down as far as my feet, so there's no chance that I'll be decorated in blue or silver or whatever is the latest shade.

As we arrived back I saw Maud and Chris walking our way. Trying not to look too interested, I waited to see if the boys had arrived. No sign. It's hard asking a question when you're trying to appear as if this isn't the most important thing on your mind.

'Cuppa?' Mum asked.

'Lovely idea,' Chris replied, looking to Maud for agreement.

Those two are so happy. I wonder if Mum has told them about Dad? About me? Probably. Dad is the kind of drama she shouldn't have shared too closely with Dora, who'll have it on the six o'clock news given half a chance before you can say 'secret'.

Just a little bit more for Ms. Wolfe to gloat over. Let it be the end of term soon.

'What time are Barry and Tyler getting in?' Mum asked.

Phew! That saved me the trouble.

'They aren't. Billie rang this morning. Tyler's seeing some specialist or other. He hasn't recovered as well as they hoped after the chicken-pox. He's very tired all the time. Maud and I are trying to persuade her to let them live with us for a while. All the rushing about travelling is fine when you're fit. We'll see.'

Christian's voice is like velvet; he has this slight accent. I like accents. Shame about Barry and Tyler though.

We're all going to watch a film in a minute. Bliss. We can stick our feet up on the coffee table, put our cups on the floor. There's no one to nag us. Sorry Dad, but I'm afraid that what you do best is moan.

1.30 . . . late, late, late, and tomorrow's Sunday and Ted and Eileen will be here, but it's back to the bathroom, safe haven during emergencies. This isn't an emergency entry, but I know I'll forget what I want to say unless I write it now. Mum and I have had a big talk. Things are bad between Dad and her. She admitted that sometimes she's tempted to walk out. Please don't. As I try to imagine what it would be like without her all I can see is darkness. She does everything. Dad sometimes tells her that she's got an easy life, no worries. Mum was explaining that it was Father Casimir who advised them to take a break for a while. Dad's used some of the redundancy money and Uncle Sean insisted on helping out. They rang the States from Father Casimir's house. I wonder if they'll pay for the call on the next collection plate. They have enough in their bank account to last them for two months. Mum rang Sean from here as well. She said that he couldn't have been kinder. That's no surprise, but then maybe she assumed he'd be as twisted and controlled and unforgiving as some of her bittersweet cronies. And Mum is thinking about finding a job. Poor Jen, we've always had Mum at home. I know it sounds really dumb, and I know that I complain about her, but she's one of those old-fashioned women who only ever wanted one thing, a house, children, and to be the best at being a wife and mother.

'I'm afraid I've not been much of a wife recently.'

I argued with her that the clothes were always clean, that the beds were made, the bathroom occasionally bleached, Jen is the picture of spoilt contentment.

'There's more to marriage than that,' she explained sadly.

I sensed the conversation was taking a turn down an alleyway I didn't want to investigate. My parents' intimate life is something I definitely couldn't explore. Their four children are evidence enough that they get together once in a while.

'One day you'll understand,' Mum sighed.

'Why do you let him bully you?'

That's what he does.

'It's his way.'

No excuse.

'When you were all small, I used to yell and shout. But you always got upset. Pleaded, you in particular Anna, 'Don't fight, Mummy.'

Oh God! Guilt, double helping. I took the fight out of my mother. I made her weak and watery. I didn't know she was fighting for survival.

'Casimir has known me all my life.'

He's white-haired, skin the colour of cement. Father Casimir is a tough prospect.

'After getting to know Matt and all those other families, I believed that at last we'd opened out to each other again.'

No way.

'It was a false promise. Your father has a huge problem with opening up, communicating. He sees the family now only in terms of being a burden, as if we're all leeching from him. That's why Casimir advised a time away, to evaluate, consider what his family really means.'

Don't hold your breath, Mum.

⟳ Eighteen

Almost the afternoon. And what a strange day so far. Sunday is always odd, restrained. First there's church. I go because it would really hurt Mum if I didn't. Sometimes I feel like standing up and shouting. NO, NO. I understand that priests are there as God's deputies. But I don't think God would have said from the pulpit, during what was meant to be sermon time, what the visiting priest said today.

'I cannot speak over that crying child.'

A woman, a very young woman, got up slowly. Absolutely everyone was watching. Old ladies with lips like string were looking; you could see disapproval like rosary beads of sweat on their smug, powdered faces. I hate make-up; the very name make-up, artifice. I like that word: artyfaces. Anyway, as she walked up from the altar to the back door there were men staring, staring. She had a little boy holding onto her skirt. The baby was so small – this was a new baby, I baby-sit, I know new when it's in front of me. Poor kid, you've only started on this crazy merry-go-round. The mother had a sleeveless dress on; eyes were darting everywhere, neighbours, school friends, mothers and fathers, contemporaries.

'Now we can resume,' he said, pompous and pious. God didn't mean for that to happen. I know it. I said it to Mum afterwards, when we got home.

'He's from the old school,' Mum protested.

Was I meant to accept that as an excuse, an explanation?

'The same old school where priests talked about unmarried mothers and had children of their own, where altar boys weren't safe, where we did as we were told? That wasn't a school, that was a prison.'

'Be quiet.' Mum banged the kitchen door shut. I could see Belle from the window sorting the sun lounger, Dave turning on the hose. Another idiot Sunday. Terry didn't have to endure Mass. He's working, he's getting sixty pence an hour. Clever Ted. User. Jenny was still asleep in her pushchair after walking home and being bored to tears listening to Mum rabbiting to everyone as we crawled back. I need a job.

'You don't know everything, Anna. There are and always will be good and bad.'

Play the violin, why don't you.

'I'm more shocked than anyone by what's happened to the Church over the last ten years. But I have faith, Anna.'

Not half.

'The Church needs the young.'

'Then why did that fool humiliate that poor woman?'

'Because he's forgotten how to be humane. He's puffed up with pride. He's wrong. But so are you. Not every priest, bishop and cardinal is wrong.'

I was about to launch into a one-sided discussion about the Pope when the phone rang. What's the use? But I prayed it was Amy anyway. It wasn't.

11.17 . . . Another day over. Good? Bad? Indifferent? Belle's snoring. Nothing new there. I saw Andrew's car parked outside the sacristy. He's back. He didn't call in. Maybe Amy'll be back at school tomorrow. Maybe not. Ted and Eileen called over with their three brats. Jenny launched their year and a half year old son off the floor. Eileen almost lost her mind. Jen's probably slipped a disc; this was a fat kid. I ate at least three and a three quarters too much. I don't ever want to have a thick waist. It's what I've noticed about women in particular. Once you get to a certain stage it's as if you suddenly billow out. I wouldn't mind a chest though; occasionally I dream of a cleavage.

No homework to do. No study to be done. I'm going downstairs for a glass of milk. BORED.

11.45 . . . I've got so used to being bored I forgot the most important, devastating, exciting piece of news. How could I? Mum asked me to go up to her bedroom to get her a cardigan, as she and Ted and Eileen and the brats were going for a walk. I leapt up the stairs two at a time. I knew that I should be clearing up, but Terry had borrowed a video from Frag. There was no way that Mum would let us watch it, she has certain actors and directors who are banned. For some unknown reason she cannot bear us watching anything with Tarantino attached to the label. Anyway, as I opened her drawer, all excited at the prospect of even more freedom, I looked out of the window. It was sad in one way because the last time I looked out of that window was with Amy. However, stretched out, brown and long and incredibly sexy, were two strange bodies on blankets. Maud's boys. I don't know when they arrived or what the news is, BUT they are here. I don't want to meet them, but I do. They'll be culture and travel and sophistication. What will they think of me? I'll go for the sick one. No I won't. I'll ignore them. Why is it so difficult to talk to some boys? I haven't even met them and already I know they'll think I'm some country hick. I'm not. I am. Oh! Forget it. I'm going to sleep.

◎ Nineteen

I'm going to write this in order of importance. I'm seething, but that's not the point. The point is that Amy and I are talking. And I'm so glad and grateful. Thankyou, thankyou, whoever restarts friendships. I don't want to deal with the seething thing right now because nothing is going to spoil the fact that I'm going over to Ollie's and Sally's tomorrow. I need to talk to Sally, need to sort out exactly what she said about my book. But even that isn't as important as my talking to Amy again. Andrew's gone. I don't care. Olivia's gone, but they're getting married in July. I can't get my head round that, nor the fact he wants me as a bridesmaid. Given time I'll have a chance to absorb some of it. His wedding. I feel shivery with excitement, not about them but us. Amy. Me.

How it all happened was so weird and yet inevitable. Ruth came bowling up to me in the corridor. She's back, she has a diamond stud in her nose and about eight rings and things in her ears. I'm not going to concentrate on the thing in her tongue because it's her body. I have to start backing off and letting people be who they are. I have to, otherwise I'll explode. No doubt Ruth will be off again soon but it was good to see her. I wish that I didn't half dislike and half adore her. Am I jealous? Is anything ever straightforward? Probably not.

'Have you seen the notice-board?' She asked breathlessly.

How can she talk round that object in her mouth? I must keep telling myself that it's not my business. It was a quarter to nine. I couldn't see what was in front of me, I didn't get to sleep for so long. How was I meant to be conscious of something written on a notice-board?

'You and Amy, you've won. I wish that I'd been here when the trials were going on.'

Well, you could have been if you hadn't been in Bermuda or London or wherever your last educational tour happened to drop you. What competition? I don't run, play basketball. I'm not bad at tennis because I just stand at the net and think spider man.

'What trials?'

'The cookery competition.'

Impossible. It was January. Amy and I entered for a laugh. She's about as fascinated by pots and pans as I am. It was an Indian dish that had to be prepared using certain oils and spices. We did a cucumber and yoghurt salad thing. Plus lentils and potato and cauliflower. I think. The meat dish was a chicken Tikka, which was easy because you had to dip the chicken in brilliant red sauce. We liked the colour. We've won our area heat and are going up to Dublin on Thursday for the finals. There's loads of prizes and we stay in a hotel, all paid for, and we're travelling with Ms. Vincent who happens to be the coolest teacher in the whole school. I don't believe I wrote that: coolest. Ugh! How childish. Ah well! I'm excited, I'm allowed and she's very young, very trendy.

Stop. That's not what I want to talk about. I've missed Amy so much. She's made me promise that never again will we allow ourselves to be overtaken by heat and hate and hormones. She's brilliant.

'Anna, 4ever friends, Amy xxx' she's written on the front cover of you, diary.

We couldn't stop talking. First things first. I'd gone with Ruth and Terry to the notice-board to check that what she was saying was true, when over the intercom came Mr. Kennedy's lispy voice.

'Will Amy Butler and Anna Fielding please come to my office.'

Terry looked as if he might hug me. He's got a face that looks as if its illuminated by a thousand lights when he smiles. He didn't hug me, because that would be too embarrassing.

I strolled down to the office. The school is falling apart. The walls are peeling paint, the floors have lino tiles that have turned-up edges like stale sandwiches. No wonder we're not allowed to run! The governors are probably waiting for one of us to break our necks and claim big compensation. Now there's an idea. Minus the broken neck. I was dreading seeing Amy. We hadn't spoken, we hadn't talked. And suddenly there she was ahead of me. All little and head down. I could tell by her shoulders that she was nervous. No wonder, she was dreading facing up to me. Am I that much of a bully? Yes, sometimes. It's not your normal bullying but, none the less, I can frighten people.

I stood back for her to go into Mr. Kennedy's office, she accidentally pushed against me. It was as if we'd touched an electric cable.

'Sorry,' we said in harmony.

I tried to smile and ended up with a twisted grin. She tried to look serious.

'Come in, come in . . .' Mr. Kennedy was beaming. 'Well done, well done, girls. This is such an honour. There are photographers coming from *The Examiner*. Such an honour.'

He babbled away contentedly, explaining we'd be staying in the Mount Holly Hotel. A hotel. I have never in all my life been in a hotel. Initially, when Mum heard, she was gambolling round like a plucked lamb. I'll get back to her. Dave is spitting with jealousy and Terry's put in an order for tapes that we can't buy down here.

Amy and I apologised, laughed. I could have cried I was so glad it was all over there's been too much aggro. My hand won't write quickly enough. Amy's told me to stop hating Olivia. I don't hate her. I don't like her, that's all. Apparently she's really nice. Nice is a word that I don't apply to people. Nice is too sweet. So, instead of bottling up that thought I said it.

'Anna.' Amy was looking severe. 'You know how much Andrew likes you, really really likes you. He respects you. You're the only friend of mine that he takes any notice of.'

I was going to remind Amy that I was more or less her only close friend but, for once, sat on my tongue.

'He knows how much you fancy him.'

Death, handy hint, please let me die at this very moment. As I'm writing I can feel my heart beating faster, my face getting hotter. I don't blush, I blow red like a geyser. As I stood trying not to look at Amy I could feel the heat rising up through my face to the tips of my scarlet hair. How? How could Andrew know how much I like him? I was too embarrassed, too ashamed. No. Not ashamed, worse, guilty.

'Would you stop.' Amy was laughing. 'It's all right. I think he's gorgeous too. But . . . He's so madly in love I'm surprised he even remembered *my* name, never mind yours.'

'Why didn't he call round?'

'We didn't have time. Mum insisted on going up to Galway. The grandparents kept inviting the world and his wife to meet Olivia. She just fits in. I don't know how, but that's what she does. She's nothing like Fleur, I promise.'

Fleur. God, what a mess she was. All 'I'm a vegetarian', and 'aren't you all terribly terribly interesting little people'. She's going to end up like Dora. Talking of Dora, she hasn't appeared for ages.

Everything felt good until Mum got a telephone call from Dad and ended up saying very firmly, 'Bob. I'm coping very well thank you. No, you don't have to come back. I'll see the bank manager.'

I was quietly pushing Fernando's old basket backwards and forwards, trying not to listen, desperate to hear. They didn't sound as if they'd parted too happily, so I hung around to lend a bit of moral support.

'Bella, Dave, bedtime!' she barked, making Jen, who was thumb-suckingly half asleep on the couch (in between her tele-viewing brother and sister) almost jump out of her Power Ranger pyjamas. It was only half ten. Normally Belle slopes round till eleven, twelve if she can swing it. There was the usual chorus of complaint.

'Now.'

Dave muttered obscenities all the way up the stairs. Mum clenched her fists, then unclenched them and went to boil the kettle. I was given the job of resettling Jen, who was totally awake and ready for a party. Wailing, sobbing, I compromised with her by putting her in my bed.

'You can take that thing right back to her room.'

Belle, still seething at the indignity of being expelled from her favourite spot, was determined to be awkward.

'Tea, Anna,' Mum called up the stairs.

Occasionally I can draw on my diplomacy reserves, my very limited reserves.

'I have two pounds. Keep Jen happy and they're yours.'

Belle's baby-blue eyes lit up like icebergs.

'Promise?'

I hate it when someone does that. I said it, I meant it. But for once I mouthed the word 'promise'.

'Just keep Jen quiet.'

As I left the pair of them I could hear Belle hissing, 'No you can't suck my blusher brush.'

She doesn't leave the bedroom to go to the bathroom at night without checking if her blusher's perfect!! That girl is a sick prophet of our future. By our, I mean us . . . GIRLS.

Mum was making us both a sandwich to go with the cup of tea. Sitting down with an almighty rush of a sigh she put her head into her hands.

'How's Dad?' I asked unnecessarily.

'Ready to come home.'

She should have been pleased.

'So, when are we picking him up?'

Mum only passed her driving test a few months ago. That's brave, learning to drive just before you get your pension.

'I'm not picking him up. I want a few more weeks.'

Deep breath, slurp of tea, silent prayer that when they do finally get back together they won't notice that I've failed every exam going. I can't study. I think transition year has sapped me of ambition.

'Sean intends to stay for a little while. He wants to

help us out, here.' Mum was grasping her mug like Jen hangs onto her armless monkey. That monkey has seen real life, rescued from halfway down the toilet, dropped on a busy road in the middle of Cork, chewed by a certain floppy hound.

'How do you mean?' And why did she look so defeated?

'He's coming home. He wants to go into partnership with your father.'

Good news, great news, generous and unselfish news. Money, safety, money is safety. No cash, no future. That's how it is. Governments change, but the truth of the matter is you need cash, to buy books, to get to college.

'Well?'

'There's no way we can stay here. Everybody knows.'

I keep going over and over what she said. How they were ashamed of him, of his past, what he represented. This is my borrowed mother, ashamed. She thinks that he'll influence Terry. Doesn't she know or understand anything? Eventually I got up and walked out, but not before I had my say. I know, I know, I've promised myself so many times not to do it, but I have to. I tumble the words. That's all.

'Sometimes I hate you, Mum. Sean's a good man.'

She raised her eyebrow. I doubly hated her for that.

'You and Dad cut him out of our lives because he never got round to becoming a priest. He explained it to me. He knew that he wasn't up to it, he didn't have a true vocation. That's brave. Then he never got round to marrying his woman, and, shock horror, she was Vietnamese. But it was because she was Vietnamese and a lot older than him that he never married. She still didn't believe that her first husband, her once young husband, was dead. Maybe he might find her. He didn't, cancer did. I don't believe it. Of all your committee and social and school and love-in friends, he wants to help. And you're ashamed. Stand up for yourself. We're almost colliding with a new millennium and you still care about all the lies and deceits and . . .'

I knew I was about to cry but she's such a fool, a liar, to herself and others. Take the issue of Margaret and the dog. Margaret had to be right. She said so, Mum conformed and forgave. Dave and the headmaster. Mum is always wrong, has to be, she believes it.

'I'd be proud of a brother who's prepared to give up his comfortable life for a family who doesn't want him. I'd be proud to know, like Dad does, just what kind of family I come from.'

Take a couple of spoons of despair, add a dash of seethe and a pinch of joy, what do you end up with? A wish to destroy. I knew I shouldn't be let loose in a kitchen! At least I've got tomorrow and Thursday to look forward to. But I also know that Sean's a good man.

PS. No sign of Tyler or Barry. Just as well, they'll hate it here. I wish I had a cheque book, my own apartment. I wish something fitted.

✺ Twenty

Tuesday, May 22nd. It's somewhere after twelve, night-time twelve. I can't be bothered looking for my clock. It's under the heap of clothes by my bed, or the books under my bed, or in amongst the washing. Later, I'll search for it later. My watch is by the sink, downstairs. Mum's talking to Dad. Again. God knows what their phone bill's going to be. However, I can't face going into the kitchen, looking at Mum looking into the distance, talking.

I feel calm, in an ecstatically miserable kind of way. I feel sick with excitement about four o'clock on Thursday. DUBLIN!!!! Yes!!

I think that I'm going to have to accept that 'The Jacob Dream' was good experience but bad writing. I went to see Sally this afternoon. She rushed at me like a Saint Bernard.

'Anna. Welcome. Forgive me. I'm so much better. I'm so sorry that Amy gave you my very bad-tempered opinion. I love your story, but . . .'

The pause was long enough to sink the *Titanic*.

'It was weeks ago. I was miserable with the pain from my back, which, by the way, is so different. Ollie says I'm a broody hen. Anyway, Amy was reading some dreadful teenage horror book. I wouldn't normally comment but . . . and I told her that she should try writing, instead of reading . . .'

Another pause. This time the QE2 hit the ocean floor.

'That even if your story was unformed at least you had taken the time and had the ambition to achieve. Amy flounced off. We're not getting on as well as we have.'

I didn't know Amy was fighting with her mum. They never fight. According to Sally, they never stop these days. More secrets.

Sally dashed about clearing a space on the table for the tea things which Amy had brought through. Firstly, Drucilla, their pet rat, who was sitting cleaning between her elegant toes, had to be chased, then caught, then re-caged with a chocolate orange biscuit for compensation. Then Seb and Colm were prised away from the television.

'Boys, you can eat without pictures to explain the process.'

Everybody talked at the same time. I was back and it was brilliant. Not once was Dad mentioned, not until I said something. Sally paused between bites of fudge cake.

No one can make fudge cake like Ollie. It's his and their son Paul's speciality.

'How's your mother? I thought I might come back. Have a chat.'

That's Baltinogar for you. A whisper is heard from one end of the place to the other. I understand why Mum's worried about Uncle Sean, I just think it's time she and Dad stood up for themselves. So once, a long time ago, he thought he wanted to be a priest. He – or God, or who cares? – changed his mind, that's all. Then he loved someone, far away, and she was far away too. And she died. That's sad. But. Now is now.

Sally drove Amy and I to our place. I excused us because I could see that Mum wanted an empty room. Terry was mixing some vile-sounding music upstairs. Dave was with him; every so often I could hear him belch into the microphone. No comment. Belle was out spending her two pounds, probably on a new blusher brush. I had had to hide the original. Jen had sucked most of it down her throat when she fell asleep. Thank God she didn't choke.

Mum trusts Sally. Grabbing the squirming youngest member of the family, with a promise of chatting to Beaky, I told Amy a bit about Maud and the boys. All the time I was nattering I could see Amy looking behind her.

'What's the matter?' I wanted to know.

'I keep expecting to see the bog beast. Normally, by this time he's tripped up Jen, eaten next door's rose bush and is belting towards Dublin with you in hot pursuit.'

'Nando's gone,' Jen explained solemnly. 'To Heaven.

Like a nangel.'

Amy didn't say anything. Then, as we were starting to go up Maud's pathway she whispered, 'I'm so sorry. We won't fight. Ever again. Promise?'

I, because I'm dumb, began to feel very sorry for myself. Tears, big like rivers, tripped off my nose. Jen was bouncing up and down, delighted to be visiting her new friends. Just as I was wiping the flood from my face the door was opened by the nearest thing to one of Jen's nangels, only this one was distinctly un-Fernando-like. I blushed, stuttered, stammered, looked halfway down his body, blushed again, tried to fix my watery eyes on his brown face, his slanting eyes, his cropped black hair. If it had been Tina meeting Jake for the first time, she would have smiled and sighed, 'Hi.'

As overweight and awkward as Tina is in my imagination, she could still have introduced herself. That's books for you!!!

I didn't. I couldn't. I stammered a bit more and then, disaster on top of chaos, Jen belted past me at three hundred miles an hour. I reached down – she's only little – and fell, straight at the feet of Tyler. Where are the cracks in the earth when you need them?

'Anna.'

Oh happy happy let-out. Christian gathered me up, placed a hand on Amy's shoulder and said. I'm shuddering inside remembering what he said. 'Come on, Tyler. You've met beautiful young women before. Meet our charming Anna and . . .?'

'Amy,' chirped Amy, unmoved, unafraid, unfazed.

The remains of the visit consisted of Amy and Jen doing all the talking. Tyler and Barry hot-footed it to our house to be introduced to Terry and Dave via Maud. I wanted to do that, show off Sally to Maud. Or the other way round. It wasn't how I meant it to be. That's all. The boys obviously thought that there could be only two rejects with Fielding for a name, so opted to test the more sensible side of the family.

When Amy and I got back, the lads were in a huddle of tapes, CDs, some of Dad's vinyl. He'll kill the lot of them if they're scratched. I said as much and got looks of such contempt from Dave, Tyler and Barry that I've decided to put myself back up for re-adoption. Amy slipped in between Terry and Tyler and looked perfect. I slouched off to do the washing-up. Maud, Mum and Sally stayed talking for ages. Back to the beginning, I haven't a clue what the time is. Sometimes I don't even have an existence, never mind a life.

Twenty-one

Let me walk you down the corridors of the **Mount Holly** Hotel. It goes on for miles; it's like being in a church, all hushed and carpeted. There are rooms to the right and left and lights, dim and bright, depending where you are. You feel important amongst the mumbling and the silences, the whispers and the slur of other sounds. This is the nearest I've ever felt to being completely alive. I mean it.

Amy and I are sharing. We've got our own bathroom, hairdryer, television – nine channels. Bliss, nine channels to choose from. There's a bar downstairs where we sat and had drinks and sandwiches last night, just after we had arrived and ditched our bags and gasped at the neat clean beds, the towels just so. No bathroom drips, clean floors, a shower and a lock, our very own lock. Ms. Vincent, call- me-Polly, drank three pints of lager. Three! She seemed fine, relaxed, happy, chatty, almost as if we'd all known each other for years. She was really funny about Ms. Wolfe. Maybe she was a bit tipsy after all.

Apparently she's going out with the werewolf's son. He's a junior doctor who sewed up her leg after she fell over barbed wire trying to escape a bull after a party. Then she proceeded to roll up her jeans leg to show us the scar – almost non-existent, I commented. That's because he should be a plastic surgeon, she informed me. The bar was packed and full of women in magazine-sleek dresses. The men were mostly in suits, some in evening gear. Oh God, they all looked good enough to eat. I was half nervous and juvenile, half fascinated by the way various people kept looking into the dark corner where we were sitting. Belle would have been absolutely perfect. It was a combination of thrilling and dangerous. I can't explain it. There was no one but Amy and Polly and me. Does that make sense? No outsider to say something bad, to spoil the moment.

Our conversation drifted from what we wanted to do in the future, to marriage, to school, then swiftly back to parties. In fact, come to think of it, a lot of Polly's conversation seemed to float round various parties. The son, Liam, sounds lovely. In fact, looks lovely; she showed us a picture. He reminds me of Dr Morrison on whom I had a crush a couple of years ago. He is now all happily married and the father of two children. I suppose I'll spend the rest of my life loving impossible dreams. Liam is in his second year as an intern; eventually he wants to do paediatrics. I hope he's an improvement on the paediatrician Jen and I had to see after our mutual meningitis share-in. Anyway, apparently Ms. Wolfe is very disapproving of Polly Vincent because she's from Limerick. Amy and I gave each other jumpy puzzled looks. Limerick is a new one on me. Even Dad hasn't found anything too much to complain about there. According to Polly, there'd been a series of articles, some time ago, about Limerick's being a dangerous place. Has Ms. Wolfe walked round certain chunks of Cork recently, I wondered. And Polly comes from a council estate. So?

'You're just not good enough,' Amy announced with a twinkle in her eye. Then she started to retell the whole miserable business about Fleur. Naturally I felt embarrassed, not so much because Fleur was a real loser, all 'I'm terribly well off, frightfully rich and aren't you funny little Irish folk a panic', but because inadvertently the story was also about Andrew.

Amy's beside me reading Mizz or More or – hang on. Let me check. No, I have done her a deep wrong, it's *Angela's Ashes*, by Frank McCourt – and she has big shiny tears in her eyes. I lent it to her having borrowed it from Mum. It's brilliant, sad and funny. Imagine rolling all those components into your first book. Kind of makes the 'The Jacob Dream' feel a bit lonely, a B movie amongst the blockbusters. And, that reminds me, I must tell Ms. Polly Vincent that Frank McCourt was originally from Limerick. Put that in your chandelier and swing on it Pat Wolfe.

The competition was terrifying; hot and terrifying; tiring, hot and terrifying. I've never seen so much chrome and glass and beautiful china dishes – mum would call it 'ware', I'd call it expensive. There were eight judges, and there were tasters and testers. I felt like a poodle at Cruft's being scrutinised, questioned. Amy stood her ground, more Yorkshire terrier than anything too exclusive. We had our photos taken before, during, after. Did you see me, birth mother? I know Mum says that you emigrated but you might be over, for the summer, in this big exciting city. Did you see our picture and wonder who the tall girl is alongside the tiny one? It's late and I'm so tired and excited I could cry. This is the time that I start to think strange thoughts. Imagine walking into a big room in a great city and just recognising her. She's about thirty-three, Mum reckons. You, Dad, you the one who made me, not the one who's busily unravelling Mum's head, maybe you're a hotel manager and you saw me today, in the lounge, in the corridor, in the lift. God, this is frustrating and I don't even know why I want to know. Because you didn't want to know me. Not at all.

Amy wants to talk. I've asked for five more minutes. She says that she can't deal with any more of *Angela's Ashes*. I was the same. She's got to the bit where the family are all living upstairs because downstairs floods during the winter. I've given Amy *Hello*. I nicked it from the lounge. Everyone in there looked rich enough to buy their own. They probably think that we're rich too, wealthy by association. HELP!!! I'm never, never going to be a snob, even if one day I do get accepted and do get on television. Where was I? I think I'm going to have a heart attack, I feel so . . . tingly, it's more than excited, it's . . . ecstasy. Hold on, future reader (just in case), I mean ecstatic, not the drug-other. I don't trust drugs, that's all. I know lots who do. Mum would die; I know that Dave has. But I also know plenty who don't. I want to stay in the don't group if I can.

We came second in the competition. I almost forgot. We did the cucumber and mint and yoghurt salad starter. Potatoes in turmeric with garlic. I know I know, it almost sounds as if we knew what we were doing. For some unknown reason, Amy and I are good at this sort of stuff. Dad wouldn't eat it even if you threatened to pickle Jen. If it's not meat and potatoes and peas or carrots, he thinks that the royal court poisoner is out to get him. The chicken was voted first of all the dishes. God knows how! At one point while I was trying to skin the poor thing I gouged a chunk out of my thumb. Blood of Anna is obviously the next thing to be marketed. But we lost points on presentation. The lemon wedges were too thick, the cucumber too uneven. I don't care, I don't care, we've got three hundred pounds to share between us. The boy who won was so shy he didn't even raise his eyes to take his cheque. I felt sorry for him, tried to make him laugh, stuck my finger in his spring roll. He didn't seem to mind. Why's everything so easy with boys you don't want?

We should have gone home this evening, but the headmaster had secretly arranged with Polly that if we

111

were placed in the top three we were to get a complete Dublin afternoon to ourselves. He can be impossible and then pleasant. Confusing. After the heat of the kitchens at the Collegiate College, where the finals were being held, we were let loose on Grafton Street, the Ilac centre, some other Italian-sounding place in Blackrock. There's everything here. I got Terry his tapes, Jenny-M a farm jigsaw from the Early Learning Centre, Dave some terrible hip-hop music with a warning that the lyrics were sexually explicit, and Belle some special tanning mousse. That girl spends too much time in the sun, she's going to end up looking like a beaten leather bag before too long. I bought Dad some cuff-links. Maybe now that Sean and he are in partnership, in what I don't know, but maybe he'll get a shirt that needs cuff-links. And I bought Mum perfume, Organza. I love having my own money. Now I know why Terry wanted a job. Having money you've earned, or won, is the best feeling. YOU DID IT. I rang Mum. She was quietly thrilled. Amy rang Sally; you could hear her screech. I rang Maud, just as Polly walked in,

'You'll need your winnings to cover the phone bill.'

She was joking. I want to live in a hotel for ever. I don't want to go home. I'm definitely coming to Dublin for college. I'd better do some work, otherwise I'll never get the grades. I'm so happy I could scream. It's all right, Amy's screaming for me. She's bouncing on the bed and yelling. If we're not careful we'll get chucked out. I can't sleep. Amy and I are going for a walk. Everything feels like music.

☺ Twenty-two

I slept for most of the car journey home. Ms. Vincent took us into a lovely pub where we ordered food. I chose a chicken sandwich because I like chicken, Amy and Ms. Vincent had soup. I wish I had. There were bits of gristle and bone in amongst the dry bread and salad. I almost choked. I chewed, I didn't want to spit it out. I thought I was going to be sick, right there in the pub. Old men were drinking pints at two in the afternoon, waitresses were serving lasagne and pies and I was quietly choking to death. I grabbed a serviette and coughed as quietly as I could into it. I could taste the rotten sandwich all the way home. Terry, Maud and Christian, you're right. There is something a bit unpleasant about meat. But I still love Mum's roasts.

Amy was dropped off first. I was dying to go in with her. I wanted to see Sally. I still haven't properly talked to her about the book. But Ms. Vincent was on her way to meet Liam. I couldn't stand in the way of true love!! We were quiet with each other as we drove back to our house. Everything was different, all the easy chat gone. That's so sad. Is it gone forever? Is she regretting being with us, free and easy?

Everyone liked their presents. Dave wanted to know even the tiniest detail. What were the shops like, the girls, the hotel, the food? I haven't seen him that interested in anything except himself, ever. Terry was tired; he'd done an extra shift at the garage. Mum doesn't know but he's saving half of everything for her. Do you know how I feel, book? It's as if all the worst news has collapsed together, right on top of me. I'm going to bed. Sometimes I really don't understand anything.

◎ Twenty-three

Saturday, June 3rd. It's freezing cold. No wonder, today's the first weekend of the summer holidays. At last!!!!!!

Sorry, sorry, sorry, diary. I haven't written for a week. Dad's home, so's Sean. He has to be the kindest man. He brought us all jeans and shirts and tiny cut-off tops for Belle and I. He kind of over-estimated the size of my chest, so I'll either have to buy a super-padded Wonder-bra, or give mine to Belle. Terry and Dave have all kinds of gear for the computer: music mixing, cartoon making, I don't know . . . tons of stuff.

So many things are happening. The very time I should have been remembering everything, too much was going on. For example, Dave should have been starting his Junior Cert on Monday but isn't. Dad and Mum, together, decided that, between glandular fever and general misery, he should repeat the year. BUT, not at our school. They're investigating, with Dave, other possibilities. Too good to be true, but it's fact.

What else? Tyler and Barry are perpetual fixtures in our house. Right now they're in Terry and Dave's room with Belle in lap-dog pursuit of them both. I can hear lots of laughter. I don't like them, they're odd. Maud keeps insisting that they're coming down. Where from? Everest. According to her they've been moved so often they find it difficult communicating. What's wrong with everybody? You just open your mouth and talk!!!

It's a pity, Tyler's so gorgeous to look at. He's tall, so tall. I know I obsess about height, but it matters to me. I wish that he'd look at me instead of through me. But why would he? He's been everywhere, seen everything, has brilliant parents and really belongs, fits in, with Maud and Christian.

Why would he look at me? The first time I appeared, I fell at his feet in my school uniform and looked like a giraffe in drag. He ignores me because he knows I'm boring and bossy, the complete big sister. No doubt Belle (who never leaves Terry and Dave's room these days, just in case she can squeeze into a conversation with either Tyler or Barry) has told him how horrible I am. And I am.

Terry reckons Tyler and Barry are 'neat'. NEAT – this from Terry. He's definitely under some transatlantic influence. And that's another thing. They sound half English,

116

a quarter American, and they occasionally chatter away in French and Italian. A bit of Cork Irish is drifting into their conversation. Luckily Dave has decided to drop the ever-present F word. According to Barry it's passé to swear!!! After all the thumps and recriminations from his parents and family, it took a couple of loafing lunatic visitors to make the difference in Dave.

There's a big worry. Tyler has some sort of blood disorder, which is why he's so knackered all the time. I overheard Mum and Maud talking about it yesterday. Jen and I were attempting to feed Beaky, who sits on the work surface glaring wickedly at the fridge door. As soon as you go to open it he flutters like a crazed chick straight onto the bottom shelf, whereupon he pokes round looking for cheese. Yes, I said it, cheese. Not for him Brie or Camembert, Edam or Stilton, the only thing he'll touch is Irish Cheddar. A bird of taste! Maud says that she doesn't worry about the hygiene issue. I do the worrying for her. Whenever she wants tea or coffee brewed for Christian, who is hot into his book – we rarely see him – I wash and rinse everything I see. I know Maud's into God and love, but there are limits.

Anyway, Tyler has this blood thing. He has to go into hospital on Monday for a series of tests. I've never seen Maud sad, but, as Jen and I were taking the bossy bird out into the back garden for a flying lesson, I saw Mum put her arm round Maud and say, 'We'll pray. There's one prayer that works, it's "Lord, I can't, You can . . ."'

I didn't hear the rest, I had to remove the bird from Jen's head.

Now my heart's in overdrive. I'm not thinking clearly, I'm afraid to. Jesus! What if Tyler's dying? No. My hand's shaking thinking about that. Send him back to his parents, please.

꩜ Twenty-four

I have four pages left, diary, plus the hard inside cover and then you are upside down and right way up filled and finished. But because this has been such a strange three months I've got to continue, all in one. It would seem like letting everything down if I change now. Christian has given me some beautiful parchment paper. I was admiring it while he was shuffling round on his desk looking for his glasses, as usual, and, as usual, they were on top of his head. I pointed to them. I didn't want to do what Maud does, pop them back on his face. That's between them.

The paper is in shimmering blues and greens, a present from his publishers.

'I'll only scribble notes on it, or Maud will use it for shopping lists. You have it. Then it will be special to me.'

He's unique. They're unique. Please don't make us

have to move. Not now. Because the sheets of paper are so big, I can fold them over and tie them in with the rest of all this.

On a boring note, Shazza's banned from our house. Again. Dora called round the other day. I can't say that I've missed her. She took one look at me as I came into the kitchen and carried on explaining why she found Sean's presence, sleeping in the front room, so terrible. Obviously diseases can be caught from good people!! It's a pity that the Doras of this world didn't get wiped out along with smallpox.

It's the summer and it hasn't stopped raining since Thursday. The garden looks like a rainforest. My hand's aching and I haven't even begun to think about all the things I want to write. Quick list. It's Tuesday June 6th and Tyler has been in hospital for two days. Dad and Mum were skirting round each other like two dogs about to have a fight this morning. They didn't. Uncle Sean and Dad have visited all sorts of agencies looking at business opportunities. Sean and he seem easy enough with each other. I asked Mum about it and she said that Sean and Dad were determined to go for a family-run business, then, in the future, there might be a job for us. She did her philosophical, sociology bit.

'It's a different world from the one your father and I understood.'

I tried to listen. I can only see now, in the present, yesterday and tomorrow give me a pain.

'There's no security, Anna. No permanence.'

There she was, cleaning the sink, smearing Jif about the draining board, something she must do in her sleep she does it so often.

'But if we have our own business . . .'

She gazed off into the distance, dynasty-building for the Fieldings, with Sean as part of the family. I like that. I must find out from Sean how he buried the hatchet and Dad came home smiling!

Belle is broken-hearted because Shazza's banned. But Toby, her limp twin, suddenly appeared today to see Dave. They are back talking to each other again. Toby and Dave are going through phase four of disagreeing with parental decisions, so the Fielding family seemed as good a cause as any to take up the fight with his parents; not that Tom, his dad, knows anything about it. He's in the army and is posted abroad. I know that's the only way he manages to stick with his wife. Dora's reasons for the moratorium (I wonder if that's the right word, it looks suitably bleak . . . and impressive!! I'll check later) are that there are unseemly influences at our house. For unseemly read Sean. No comment. Dora inspires loathing, something bordering on hate, but more often than not she exhausts me. I told her. Mum and Dad didn't even try and stop me. She's a dyed-blonde snob with a BMW bank account and a dodgem car for a brain. No doubt she'll embroider that comment at one of her fund-raising coffee mornings. Do I care? I don't think so.

Details. No, firstly, still no news about my book. That's not news, Anna, that's reality. Tyler has had so many tests, according to Maud he should be about ready to sign up for the next space programme. Nobody knows what's wrong with him. I could always give Polly Vincent a ring, see if her Liam has anything to do with Tyler. Amy and I called up to see him yesterday. It wasn't my idea. He's in a small room with two other guys – both are really old and confused. I can't describe what effect this is having on Tyler. All the dark healthy skin has faded. He looks thin and hardly talked. Amy has absolute faith in her ability to cheer people up and she fancies Barry. Poor old Terry. But he doesn't seem to notice. However, she was hoping Barry would be sitting by the sick-bed. It didn't happen. Amy assumes that everyone's like her family, a quick natter and a few homemade biscuits and, hey presto! back to normal. I of course was mortified, firstly because I was wearing button-up jeans and had forgotten to button the last three. I don't suppose Tyler noticed, he didn't seem that interested in anything. He did ask Amy to get hold of some Terry Pratchett books; Seb and Colm have them all so that's fixed. I met his mum, Billie. It was like being introduced to a celebrity; she carried fame with her, if you know what I mean. She walked into the room just as I was trying to persuade Amy to leave. Amy had settled in for the winter with Tyler's grapes and a long discourse about Andrew's wedding. You could see that Tyler was riveted by his closed eyes.

I looked up as the door opened. Billie has brown hair, long, caught up at the back with a claw comb. Straggly bits fell down on either side, they were brown and silver.

That takes guts. Not dyeing your hair when it's going grey must take real courage. Mum's been every colour from brass to black, she even tried red once just to keep me in the picture. Anyway, as Billie walked in, high-heeled sandals, long floaty white skirt and a shirt, I knew that maybe my real mother might look like that. I longed for Billie to tell me that she, once upon a time, gave a baby away. Crap! Sorry, book. But sometimes all that's left are dreams.

She went over to Tyler and stroked his head. He opened his eyes and looked really angrily at her.

'How are things, darling?' Then noticing us, 'Hi, I'm Billie, thanks for keeping Tye company.'

You could see that Tyler was unimpressed. I was the one who wanted to brush against her rich easy manner. She oozed . . . I'm not even sure what it was. Class? Style? Can't explain it.

'When's Dad getting here?' Tyler sat himself up and rubbed a hand against his jaw. There was a scratchy sound; he has a dark beard growing. I'm so sorry, book. He is heart-thumpingly gorgeous, even when he's glaring at his beautiful parent and ominously unimpressed with me.

'Shall I organise a shave for you?' Billie asked, looking concerned, scrambling around for somewhere to dump her giant bag, plus magazines tucked under her arm. But totally ignoring Tyler's question about his father.

It was time to leave. Tyler and his mother were talking quietly but heatedly as we shut the door. Amy reckons that Tyler is a gift from the gods of fiction, that I ought to pen the next romance around him. Only, she insists, he has to die. Too near the truth for my liking. Mum told me that they think he has something like M.E. Apparently it's a funny, almost unknown disorder that leaves you really tired all the time. Permanent flu. He certainly looked that way. But – good news – it shouldn't kill you.

After Amy and I got back, we dried ourselves off, ate hot chicken sandwiches and drank all the red lemonade that Maud had dumped in the fridge. Her grandsons didn't like it; hurray for their bad taste. Amy and I went for a stroll round the Park. The rain had taken a temporary break, plus the big house at the entrance gates is finished and there was another removal van. We decided to go the long way round. I wanted to buy some Spice Girl stickers for Belle; she's been so depressed minus Shazza, I almost feel sorry for her. Walking into the shop I noticed how empty the shelves were, as if there's been an alien invasion (they forgot to beam me up) and that, under siege, the shop was dying away.

'Hi, Mr. Eglinton,' I said cheerily. He smiled. He's a good guy. I bought three sets of stickers and was going to walk out without saying anything when his daughter charged in from their house next door and announced, rudely I thought, 'They don't have any packers at Pheeny's and Wright.'

Amy and I looked at each other knowingly. Hey, we've followed the influx of just about every removal van from here to Bangkok. Well, not quite, but Dublin, Waterford, Birmingham and Manchester have been well-represented. Mr. Eglinton raised his hand to silence her.

'You're not going?' Amy was genuinely upset. There's something special about local shopkeepers – well, some local shopkeepers.

Mr. Eglinton had a whispering chat with the daughter, Lizzie, who left pretty rapidly looking cross. She always looks cross, nothing new there.

'I'm quietly letting everything run down, stock, etc.' That was obvious.

'We're actually getting to go to our little paradise in the Dordogne. Lizzie never settled. And she doesn't like the boys' accents.' He looked apologetic as he said that. Dora, you have a friend, you and darling Elizabeth would make a perfect pair!

'So, I'll be putting this place on the market soon. There's already an interested party.'

I tingled with excitement. I didn't even have to ask. For 'interested party' think Arthur O'Conor. Suddenly Amy and I took flight, after a big thank you and hope the sale goes well. It was time to motivate Dad and Sean. They, no doubt, wouldn't know anything about any of this because dear Arthur O'Conor is so busy slipping and sliding expanding his empire, greasing palms, he doesn't wholeheartedly remember the rules. For once God, let us, the Fieldings, win. I don't care about the book, the tan, being shortened by a couple of feet, I want the shop for Dad.

I forgot. Please make Tyler well – and maybe, perhaps, make me look interesting enough for him to want to talk to me. Please.

⟲ Twenty-five

So this is what June looks like. The river burst its banks and overflowed onto the new road. Cause of catastrophe: rain, a bit more rain and then a cloudburst. Come back April, all is forgiven. The garage forecourt, Ted's garage, Terry's garage, was flooded. Terry is delighted, he had to work from seven in the morning helping to clear up the debris. More lovely money. I pity all the poor tourists who've started to arrive. According to Terry, any of them who stop off to fill up are delighted. They arrive knowing that it might be wet. Misguided fools. Hand me just a little bit of sunshine weatherman.

Got a postcard from Ruth. Odd. Very odd. She's temporarily holidaying in Switzerland, which she maintains is for the Gnomes. Whatever that means. And she said that by Christmas she's going to have a brother or sister. Obviously wires are crossing all over the place. I was about to show my postcard to Amy when she handed me hers, exactly the same message. Weird. Ruth mixes with some pretty odd types, does stuff that I wouldn't dream of doing. It's not that I'm good but I am afraid.

'She'd probably been drinking tequila slammers,' Amy announced matter-of-factly. I let out one of my don't understand sighs, which prompted Amy to slap me over the head with Belle's disposed-of jelly shoe. After that we went browsing in the shopping centre, having had a twenty-minute wait in the rain for the lousy bus. No comment. I've probably got brain rot and the bus company doesn't care.

When was my last entry? Hold on. OK, it was Tuesday, now it's Friday. I'm not deserting writing, simply not doing very much at all. Reading, all the time, rubbish and classics and anything I can get hold of. We rented *Romeo and Juliet*. Bliss, double bliss, too brilliant. It's the biggest film I've ever seen. I mentioned to Sean that I loved the music. Lo and behold, I have Radiohead playing in the background. He's another angel!!!

I've decided that Margaret is completely, not partially, deranged. If I ever write another book I'll use her as a brown-rice, macrobiotic cereal killer. The full account.

I baby-sat for her a couple of days ago. She was off to all sorts of farewell drinks parties.

'Kerry's back in Dublin. I'll be joining him soon,' she trilled, squashing cream blusher over her cheeks. The mirror in their hallway is kind of harsh; as I walked past she looked like Dracula's after-dinner minx. Adam and Chloe were really acting up. Unusual, I thought. After she'd left, I stuck all their toys into a holdall and took the children to our place. It's only a few doors away, so, no, I didn't leave a message on the answering machine, or leave a note. I assumed she'd be late home and that the little ones would be safely tucked up in their own beds. Don't know why. I definitely didn't assume she'd panic.

Mum, Dad and Sean were sharing a bottle of wine in the kitchen when I got home.

'Jen around?' I asked.

Dad tossed his head towards the TV room, where Belle was ensconced with Barry. Now that was a surprise. But, as she told me later, banging at her blonde locks with a brush, he'd only sat beside her because he was waiting for Dave and Terry. Terry wasn't back from work and Dave, plus Toby, were continuing to annoy Dora. They deserve a medal! For once I can see an improvement in Dave's behaviour. Oddly enough, I'm kind of grateful to have started this new diary. You feel friendly, book, even if you were invented out of anger. I must check my first diary soon. I hope it hasn't been eaten by mice.

Anyway, Adam and Chloe, who used to be prime examples of perfect hand-rearing, shoved and pushed and made Jen cry. Not an easy thing. Jen cries because you won't read to her, or give her extra ice cream. Normally, if you knock into her, or, as has been known, give her a thump, she responds by thumping you back. Whatever Adam said or did, or Chloe for that matter, Jen did a major Niagara and Mum told me it was time to take my charges home. I'd probably been away from their house for two hours max. As I walked Adam and held Chloe, I was vaguely aware of flashing lights, a police van. Strange, a bit more activity than usual on a Saturday night.

'Oh thank God, thank God.'

Margaret rushed at me as if I were a vision from Heaven. She was kissing Adam, who was about as rapt as Tyler had been when his mum was fussing him. Chloe clung onto me and refused to move. My parents, looking out of the window, witnessed the commotion and came running out accompanied by Maud, who'd obviously popped into ours to get away from the noise of Christian's computer.

Oh blast!

'Coming, Mum'

I'm needed downstairs.

It's half past one in the morning. I'm trapped in the bathroom, with torch, again. I daren't let Dad know I'm here. He's almost human tonight; can't break the spell.

The upshot of all the drama is that Kerry has gone back to Dublin, but sort of without his wife and with a girl he met at the Art College here. They're off to Sydney or somewhere and he wants the children. This is sad, genuinely sad. He's looking for a divorce because he says that Margaret's a controlling compulsive parent. I can't argue with him, but I do feel sorry for the whole lot of them. Margaret sobbed out her tale of woe while I brewed tea for her and Mum and Maud. Margaret's due to leave at the end of next week. She's going to the Cotswolds, in England, because that's where her mum lives. They've been spending a few nights at Maud's. I don't know whether to believe this, knowing what Margaret's like. But, apparently, Kerry fully intends to kidnap the children. Which is what she thought had happened when she came home to get her credit cards, which she'd forgotten. Finding the house empty, she tried to ring ours, got the unconnected tone and thought the worst. We have been temporarily disconnected because we couldn't afford the bill. Only the mobile is on the go. How would she know something like that? Mum still buys flowers from the supermarket to prove we're all drowning in cash. Impressions, mustn't let the side down, everything has to appear perfect. I'd corkscrew out of my head trying to remember who knew and who didn't know all the details of our, hopefully, soon to be averted poverty and collapse. And Margaret was playing the same game. Pretending that she and Kerry were still a happy family. A little bit of truth goes a long way.

My new prayer is, I will allow myself to grow to six feet, be ignored by Andrew for the next ten years – he doesn't want me anyway. I will do anything. Please, please let us get the shop. I'll work, for nothing, I'll scrub floors. It can rain until the year two thousand. WE NEED THE SHOP.

Tyler's due home tomorrow. They've found nothing positively wrong with him. Maud says it's psychological. Great, no doubt all my hair will drop out overnight I'm so psychologically disturbed. Maybe the praying thing helped as far as Tyler is concerned. I hope so. I pray a lot of the time even when I know it's not a real prayer or a real possibility that certain things might change. Terry's convinced that there can't be a God. Now that he's grazing with the veggies he believes that only man could have created all this bleakness. Too deep for me. I'll go with God and angels, fifty-fifty chance and all that. That's what Grandmother Luckmore said to me before she finally went into never-never land.

'Take your chances, Anna. There could be and there mightn't be. Either way, believing is much more comforting.'

Granny L doesn't know any of us any more. Don't forget her, God, just because she's forgotten you. She's eighty-seven and used to be a nursing theatre sister in the Second World War. I've seen pictures of her looking like a model, holding kittens, feeding a duckling. She's told me some of the stuff she was involved in when prisoners of war weren't getting enough rations. I haven't forgotten you, Granny L. One day I'll research and write your story. This is a true promise.

Twenty-six

Just another Sunday? It wasn't. It's the eleventh and after Mass Jen and I planted sweet peas on Fernando's grave. They seemed appropriate. Sean cooked pasta. Dad looked at his plate cautiously; I think he assumed the pasta squiggles were about to leap up and choke him. Mum is wearing make-up, has cut her hair very short with wispy bits round the sides and long at the back. She's lost weight. Tell me she isn't being my long lost Tina. Tell me that she isn't just a little bit more than fascinated by Sean. The problem is that he's . . . exciting, easy-going, funny, he listens, he waits, doesn't interrupt. He has money and is generous. He's the opposite of Dad and I'm being stupid. But there is something going on in this house. I tried to talk to Terry about it but he was too preoccupied counting his cash and asking me to deposit money in the Credit Union.

'If I can give them a couple of hundred.'

Sweet dreams. Slave-driver Ted doesn't think overtime's a good idea. Therefore, when Terry does an extra twenty minutes, half an hour, three quarters, clever Ted gets it for nothing. That's exploitation.

'Terry. Look at Mum. Really look at Mum.'

He stopped doing sums on the back of Dave's girly magazine – I'll get rid of it later.

'Anna. She's almost fifty.'

'So?'

She's not, she's not even forty-five. We're imagining it, I'm imagining it. She isn't confiding in me. OK, confiding meant no sleep and E grades for most of my subjects, but at least I had a clue. She isn't confiding in me because I can hear them, Sean and her, talking late into the night. Help! One minute it's divorce, her working, Dad leaving. Now it's Mum running off with Sean. Brain. Give me a break. Give them a break.

I couldn't believe it, Polly and Liam called round this evening. The pretext was photographs from the competition; the truth, Liam wanted an intro to Christian. I nattered on about Maud and Christian in the hotel to Polly who told Liam who went into overdrive because Christian isn't only a photographer naturalist, he's also a biochemist who conducted all sorts of research into native Indian medicines. More mysteries. They probably all sit naked smoking peace pipes. Is it any wonder that Barry and Tyler have head problems? Wish I was one of their head problems.

I waltzed Polly and Liam round to Maud's. I was dying to ask him about his lupine mother, the SHE WOLF. But manners always get in the way of truth. We were accompanied by the dreaded Jen, who was getting well in the way of Dad's and Sean's business plan. To get the stretch of things they'd spread out huge sheets of paper with projections and lists and heaven knows what else. I should have done business studies. Whatever, Jen was sitting on most of it sucking a dripping lolly, not because it was hot but because she insisted on holding the stupid thing with her hand, avoiding the stick. Crazy kid. Never, not ever, am I going to have a Jen.

Got another odd postcard from Ruth, as did Amy. All it said was, it's a girl. Amy and I have decided she's drinking something stronger than tequila. We all know that her mother can't have any more children, that Ruth's a bit of a miracle; for miracle read mistake. However.

Maud was delighted to see us all. Tyler was in meltdown with his mum. Billie and he were sitting in the big room, the squashy furniture room, as Maud brought us through.

'Company, darlings,' she announced emphatically.

I've been there, seen the sullen faces, know the next move, it doesn't need a joypad or a mouse to know that this is a hands-on, shoot-'em-out game. Billie didn't look stressed, she looked battered. Tyler got up and walked towards the door.

'Say hullo, Tye,' his mother insisted.

He shut the door between him and company so hard

that the blue glass vases on the mantlepiece jingled. I wanted to go and talk to him. I've seen Dave in that mood.

Thinking about Dave reminds me that Barry was on the missing list. I had information on Barry's whereabouts. He and my beloved second brother were in town on a hoochie hunt. My apologies, book, for hoochie, read girl, for hunt, ignore the possibilities. If it's possible, Barry is even more juvenile than Dave. I keep telling Amy that dark coffee eyes, nature-bleached blond hair and a slim body to die for is no reason to start wearing skirts that aren't big enough to blow your nose on and cropped tops that will have you in an emergency room before you say bronchitis, never mind pneumonia. But, Amy continues to be blissfully obsessed.

'Liam, I'm so sorry ...' Maud, wearing a large woollen hat and at least three heavy-knit sweaters, served us all tea and coffee. She was upset. Tyler? The fact that Margaret is still with her? Margaret looked wired. Most probably the strength of the engorged caffeine count. Margaret used to have everything decaffeinated. Maud's taught her a trick or two over the last few days. The woollen hat was in reference to the cold, the jumpers because the oil hadn't arrived and so there was no heating. Tip the giant olive oil container into the tank, I wanted to yell. Come on, Tyler, talk. Stop beating your mum up with words. I know I'm boring and plain and big. But I do a great line in listening.

Anyway, Sunday, Polly, Liam, Billie, Maud. There was

a large coal fire, plus the Stanley stove blazing in the kitchen. No wonder Tyler was in meltdown, the place felt like a reptile house.

Christian was in London, hence all the apologies. Liam was genuinely disappointed. There's some tribe or other who have an incredible success rate with premature babies. I kind of got bored after that, went in search of Beaky and Adam and Chloe. Jen, fearlessly, was standing in the converted bird room with Beaks sitting about a centimetre from her eye.

'Jen,' I called softly.

This bird could have your eye out like a pea from a pod without counting.

'Put Beaky down.'

Beaky squawked, Jen stroked his lush blue-black feathers. Chloe tottered over to them, the bird fluttered, I freaked. Margaret, hearing the commotion, arrived and ran off with Chloe.

'Hey. What about my sister?'

Forget it. Jen was soothing the irritable fowl syndrome. Maud appeared, she could have been looking for an early morning pair of socks, that's how concerned she was.

'Jenny.' Clapping her hands she watched and waited while Beaks took off to the window ledge. 'Don't you think it's time we taught Beaky to fly, properly fly. Maybe he'll even make it up to the big trees.'

Jen was impressed, so was Adam, so was I come to think of it.

It's only now I realise what a sacrifice Maud was making. She and Beaky were night and day companions. And, because Margaret was freaking out downstairs about estranged husbands and kidnappers and wild animals in houses, Maud was prepared to take action. We all trooped off into the garden, all except Tyler, who was a shadow watching us from the bedroom.

Maud and Christian have only been here for a few months but their garden is already a magical pond, a clump of trees, big shrubs, flowers, colour, lights to tempt moths. One day I'll learn all about it. One day. But there's so much. How can it happen when there's so much to learn?

We stood near the bird table and Maud stroked Beakie's tail feathers.

'Look, Jenny, strong feathers.'

Feathers to you or me, book, but if he didn't have those feathers he couldn't fly. That funny little smelly thing I'd witnessed all those weeks ago was about to be set properly free. And I could feel tears prickle behind my older sister routine. Did you say to me when I was six weeks old, now you can go. I've seen you, I know you, I believe you'll be fine. Did you, birth mother?

Beaky flew like a dream. I dreamt.

✺ Twenty-seven

10.45 am. *It's happened. Tyler's taking me to the* cinema this evening. Don't know what we're going to see. I've been so wrapped in breakups and downs, I haven't a clue what's what in the world of entertainment. I'm rigid with fear. This is so ridiculous. I've always promised myself that I'd never be one of those dumb females who get all breathy and stupid about a guy. And I'm doing it. I gave Amy a call; she's organising wedding stuff. What's to organise from here? Lots, apparently. The cake is going to be a Butler confection, plus, at some point, Sally's making the bridesmaids dresses. Do I want to be a bridesmaid? Hell, I don't know. Make me interesting. More later. HELP!!!!

11.10 pm. It's late. It's always late. Already it's the sixteenth of June and I suppose tomorrow will happen. Tyler was fine; in fact, good company. He explained how embarrassed he was but that, seeing as his mother and grandmother insisted he get out, I was as good a reason as anyone. I didn't have much to say. The film was a film. The popcorn and Coke were popcorn and Coke. I met up with people from school, introduced some of them to Tyler. He showed particular interest in Catherine O'Conor; yes, boss of the year Arthur O'Conor's daughter. She's an airhead, a five foot two inch airhead, and he asked me for her phone number. I told him to use the telephone directory like anyone else would. He said goodbye. And that's it. Maybe tomorrow I'll find something important and earth shattering to say apart from the fact that it's raining. How come you can guarantee during exams that the sun shines like a fool and, as soon as holidays come, Mr. Freeze takes a stroll round your Park? Why do I build my hopes up?

Twenty-eight

Sorry about the blank days, book. I don't want to waste my precious parchment pages on trivia. Sean and Dad are way down; deep depression. The Eglinton's shop has possibly gone to the highest bidder. Guess who? I wish he, his wife and Catherine and all the other O'Conors would take a hike to Kuala Lumpur. It won't happen. But, today, Monday the eighteenth of June, I know one thing for certain: I am not going to be a bridesmaid. I refuse. Mum says that it's an honour. Huh! Is she being asked to wear a baby-blue confection that looks as if it's been rejected from a nineteen seventies pantomime? I told Sally I'm not doing it. I'd walked into the village with Dave, Toby and Barry to check out the notice on this Saturday's disco. I'm not going, but Dave and Barry continue to scout for talent. Sally, driving past, spotted us and slowed down.

'Can you come over a bit later on? Olivia's sent some pictures of bridesmaid's dresses. I want to know what you think.'

As soon as she'd gone, Dave and Barry started to describe what sort of dress they would like their particular bridesmaid in. I closed my ears to them and kept plodding. The sun has found its way back to our small patch of paradise. Just as well. Our house is on the market. The sign sits solemnly on the neatly cut grass at the front. Our house isn't ours any more. It's clean and smells of air freshener and bubbling coffee grounds. Mum read somewhere that the smell of freshly ground coffee increases the chances of a quick sale. Whatever happens, we're going to move into a rented place. Just as well that Fernando has a place in heaven. I hate to leave him and Bimbo behind. Better not mention to the prospective buyers that we have our own animal graveyard; then we'd never get shot of the house.

Christian's back, he's signed a deal and is going to be published for the Christmas season. That's too far away when you don't even know where you're going to be living. Maud and he really missed each other. I was in Mum's room trying to find a scrunchy for my hair, which I ought to cut but can't be bothered. Mum collects elastic bands, scrunchies, on her daily cleaning round. All this organisation is unnerving; she's turning into a Stepford wife. Anyway, as I was hunting on the dresser top (no dust) I looked out of the window and Maud and Christian were doing the rounds of shrubs and bushes, arm in arm. Beaky, circling above them, completed the picture. Although he's been set free, he reappears two or three times a day to be fed. Clever bird.

I couldn't face going over to Maud's after the Tyler incident. I felt used. But she's been helping Mum out. Billie has left the boys, who will return to England and the dad's studio in September. Good riddance. By the sound of things their family is as imploded as ours. Tyler (poor baby) feels neglected. Oh yeah!! He's about to attend the most private of colleges, go to whatever university he chooses and HE feels neglected.

⊙ Twenty-nine

Saturday. Just Jen and me. The disco-goers are disco-
going. Dad, Mum and Sean are out to dinner. Terry is
working. Amy has gone away for a few days. All the family's energies are going into planning this wedding thing.
It's going to be small, according to Sally. Right. Small.
The idea is we all fly out on July 8th. That bit's exciting.
Olivia's family home is in Cambridge. I've seen pictures
and programmes about Cambridge. It looks beautiful.
The church is a tiny chapel, enough room for fifty people. Then the reception is in the Hogan Centre, whatever
that is. Amy is taking it all in her stride. I oscillate
between delirium at going to England and fear about the
cost. I tried asking Mum, but she gave me this new
enigmatic look and said it was all going to be fine. That's
what she keeps doing recently, smiling a secret smile. I

know I read too much into everything, but my mother is beginning to look positively young. She weighs about nine stone. I want the old Mum back. She's bought this beautiful dress and jacket for the wedding, it's in a burnt orange colour. Six months ago she'd have considered long and dowdy and been happy with it. This dress is short and snappy. My mother has rediscovered her legs. SCARY.

Jen's coughing upstairs. More of nothing later.

◎ *Thirty*

I'm so sorry, pages, so sorry. I'm shivering and laughing and . . . halt. Did I ever believe that what has happened could have happened. No. Where are you Anna? Sitting at a very elegant little table in the garden of Maud and Christian's. Beaky is basking on the bird table, the sun is out and the umbrella is up. Christian insisted, said that my precious paleness must be protected. I die, I swoon. No. That's Tyler's department. He is lying beside me, reading. We didn't sell our house, it kind of burnt down; not all of it but enough. There I was describing Mum's outfit and upstairs was beginning to crackle and burn. Ages ago I mentioned a funny smell in the attic. That was no funny smell, that was occasionally over-heating wires. I also mentioned mice and sewing machines, that was also to do with the electrics. The whole place was faulty. There's

145

going to be a court case. God knows what happens in between because everything is up in the air. But, according to Sean, the insurance is fine, the builders are liable. Joke. Our builder went bankrupt – I think it's almost expected in Temple Manor. Dad and Mum and the others are renting Margaret's old house. Nobody's heard from Margaret since she left. I miss the baby-sitting cash and have taken to reading Mr. Men books to Jen because I got quite fond of Adam and Chloe. I wonder what Kerry is doing? About him I don't care but Margaret and the littles, I hope they're all right.

Half of me doesn't want to remember the fire, it was so nearly a disaster. Tyler is disappearing, more cold drinks. Maybe now I can concentrate!

When I went to investigate Jen, she was sitting on the landing plus blanket and monkey. She explained quite logically that there were lights in her room. It was only then that I noticed a filmy coat of smoke seeping around us. And the lights were glowing embers above her. I thought she was a thick kid. She went up in my estimation. I didn't panic. I carried her downstairs and straight to the Anderrsuns – Jen, without being asked, grabbed you, book, as we passed through the kitchen. Christian phoned the fire brigade and Maud cuddled Jen, who was delighted to be up and about at ten o'clock at night. I insisted on going back. The fire was mainly upstairs at that point and I knew that there were certain things that Mum would be empty without; the photograph albums, her radio. Not clothes and things, but all those irreplaceable bits that are the past. Christian was on the phone and I was feeling like superwoman. But Tyler followed me.

'Don't be so stupid. Don't go back in.'

I tried to explain as I choked through the kitchen that I had to do what I had to do. He threw out an angry comment that I seemed to be of the opinion that the whole world relied on me to sort out the mess. I ignored him. Then I remembered my tissue diary. I know. Madness. Now I know, real madness. Upstairs was beginning to fall about, collapse. But once I had the albums and a few other things in the back garden, I rushed back in. IDIOT MOVE.

There were proper flames by this time, and I was really frightened. Tyler pulled me back, but I had to find the suitcase. Maybe it was the fumes. No, it was much more than that. The tissue diary was about me, and there's so much of me that I don't know about that I couldn't lose any more pieces. Tyler gave me a thump, then I started to cry. I had to get the diary. He was dragging me downstairs when, out of nowhere, a ceiling began to fall apart. The case, the old leather case, scorched, mighty hot, fell on top of Tyler's back. He fell.

It was suddenly slow-motion time. I could hear yelling and shouting outside. No fire engine, the fire people have to come from the city. Suddenly I realised what I'd done, how I'd endangered someone. Dropping the case, I dragged Tyler out. He lay in the front garden completely still. I have never been so frightened in my life. I thought he was dead. I bent down to give him mouth to mouth. No joke, when someone isn't breathing and they look dead, you don't remember anything but the fact you can help. We'd studied all about resuscitation in First Aid classes. Thank you transition year. I definitely wouldn't have bothered otherwise; I mean, First Aid is pretty dull. But it's not, it's vital. Out of nowhere Dr. Morrison appeared. I was sobbing. Guilt is a heavy companion. Tyler was covered in soot and so still. Maud, holding Jen with Christian standing beside her, waited silently. No hysterics, no shouting or recriminations. And Tyler lay there. The house was beginning to look like Tara in my mind, and I wanted to fade away. The tissue pages that meant so much now meant absolutely nothing. I suddenly knew that no treasures, no mementoes were worth what I'd done.

Tyler began to cough. It was like Christmas, turning the lights on. He tried to sit up. And I got down on my knees and did what I do best – had a really good cry.

I can't describe the last few days because I've never known what it feels like to be this happy. I know it's not permanent and I know ... That's a lie, book. I don't know anything. Except that somewhere inside me is a grin as wide and as deep as the Pacific. I keep wanting to write poetry, bad poetry. Things like:

Nice boy,
Sweet face,
Quite kind,
I like you.

Tyler loves that one. He thinks I'm a genius. That was one of the reasons he wouldn't have anything to do with me. Maud and Christian kept going on about me, so much so that he had lodged in his brain that he was inferior. He believes I saved his life, even though I regularly remind him I did exactly the opposite. I was the stupid one. Tyler has real problems concentrating. He wants to be an archaeologist, but reckons that he'll be lucky to be one of his father's backroom boys. I still haven't met Henry, but I don't like the sound of him. According to Tyler, he's always reminding him of how hard his life was, how the music business isn't easy and that, if Tyler doesn't grow up soon and grow out of whingeing about his health, he'll end up on Social Security because the dad isn't going to support him. If I get to meet him then maybe he'll listen to me; if whatever is wrong with Tyler is this M.E. thing then it takes time, sometimes a very long time, to get well.

His other problem is that Billie keeps disappearing to foreign places and dumping Barry and Tyler with friends, or in boarding schools. I suppose she's a bit like Ruth's mum, always on the gorgeous glamorous move. Wait a moment, that was how Ruth's mum used to be.

HEADLINE NEWS. Talking about Ruth, she's back, they're all back, with an extra surprise in tow. Ruth wasn't wandering out of her mind in amongst the Swiss mountains. She does have a baby sister. They've adopted a little Chinese girl, Louise. She's beautiful and Ruth and her mum are sickeningly happy. I can't believe it. Ruth's mum looks like one of those Madonna pictures and Lou-Lou, as she has inevitably been rechristened, is a stunner. Another little me. Another empty page. Except that Louise will never know her parents; her documentation says that they are both dead. I think, perhaps, that might be easier. But she has relatives out there somewhere.

10 pm. Tyler was reading over my shoulder for the last bit and told me to stop. He says that I'm too preoccupied with mysteries, that I'm lucky to be the founder of my own destiny. Then I went back to the tissue book and discovered that, ages ago, Sally had said the same thing. The tissue diary is a miracle – that old leather suitcase that used to belong to my grandfather during the war, it didn't burn. In fact the fire brigade saved most of the bottom of the house. The television, video; even Fernando's basket was saved, a bit crispy but functional. Dad has said that, when we're finally sorted, we can have another dog, a small dog. Maybe.

So this is what it feels like.

◎ Thirty-one

July 8th. The Cambridge European Hotel. Plush. I like plush. An aeroplane journey, another hotel. I can't believe it. Leaving Tyler at the airport hurt. Genuine pain. But the flight, except for the throbbing-ears bit, was brilliant. Amy and I were sitting together. I decided that this is my future. Do they take giraffes as air hostesses? Tyler keeps insisting that I don't see myself in the mirror, he says that I'm like an anorexic complicating the picture. No. I don't think so. Tomorrow we're exploring. Terry, Belle, Dave and Jenny-M are with Sean, in the rented house. Dad and Mum are downstairs having a quiet drink. Dad looks happy, as if he's hugging a secret. Still no news about the shop. But I'm not going to twist my head with that. Cambridge. I have arrived.

✺ Thirty-two

Funny day to have a wedding, on a Tuesday. But that's what happened. It still feels like July 10th but really it's tomorrow. Too confusing. All I know is that it's very early in the morning and I'm tired and happy and laughing and . . . being a bridesmaid was not all that bad. Olivia wore a tiny white lace dress; no veil, just flowers. I hate to admit it, but she looked good. Amy and I did our thing, in our baby-blue, identical, short lace dresses. I almost died — as we walked behind Olivia, somebody wolf-whistled. I looked round and it was Paul, Andrew's and Amy's brother, giving me a most impure once-over. Then I held my head up and decided to be the bridesmaid and forget about being me. We drank champagne; that was so incredible. I only had two glasses and began to bubble and babble. Amy took me outside to calm down. I couldn't.

I talked on and on and on. Everybody should be this happy.

Olivia's mum, upon whom I thought Andrew was fixated, is a fantastic person. There must be a bunch of character-types in heaven: some like Mum, a bit meek, some like Dora, gross, and some like Maud and Sally and now this new woman. She's invited Amy and I to stay. Maybe we will. Something really strange happened. I still love Andrew, but in exactly the same way as I love Terry. Where did all that passion go? Will I end up feeling about Tyler the way I feel about Andrew? God, I hope not. No wonder people keep separating. They must just go off each other. Maybe falling in love is a hoax.

Thirty-three

July 16th. 2.00 pm. Dad, Mum and Sean are in a huddle in the kitchen. The telephone rang very early this morning. The bank. We were told by the parents to go anywhere as long as we weren't around. Nice. I took Jen over to Maud's, dumped her and went for a walk with Belle, who is like a burst bubble. Barry is going out with one of the girls from the village, Toby ignores her and I have a boyfriend.

'It's not fair. You don't even bother to wash your hair.'

I could have strangled her, but love takes your mind off murder.

'You always wear the same clothes.'

She couldn't believe the wedding photos. Amy and I had both had our hair done at the hairdressers. I don't often go, because I can't think of anything more boring

⟡ Thirty-four

Sunday, the 22nd I think. I don't want to think. I'm empty. Sick with dread. Dave and Barry got into a fight. Not true. Barry got into the fight and Dave tried to bail him out. Barry had an ashtray thrown at his head, Dave a bottle. Mum and Dad are at the hospital now. Tyler rang to explain; the police had called Maud's. Mum and Dad are in bits. Mum, who has been looking like somebody has taken her over, someone new and hopeful, went pale and staggered. Dad and Sean helped her to sit down.

'I'll get the car. Bob, you look after Nickie.'

It's as if we've always lived together, always shared our lives. I want to know what's going on but I'm in charge. Terry's just got in from work and is cycling to the hospital. Don't let him get hurt. Please. Jen, sensing that something is very wrong, is half on and half off my knee, staring at the television and not really watching. Belle isn't here. Since she and Shazz got back together they've been inseparable. Was Toby with Barry and Dave? Let them be all right.

New bathroom. Margaret's old house but the same routine – me trying to write and concentrate and remember. Barry was allowed home; the ashtray didn't break till it hit the floor. No concussion, but a warning from the police. He started the fight. Idiot. Dave's story isn't so good. He's being assessed overnight; there is a lot of glass in his eye. I feel ill thinking about it. Tomorrow, when he's stabilised, they are going to operate. Mum didn't come home. Neither did Terry. Dad and Sean are downstairs. The odd thing was that they seemed more concerned about Mum than they did about Dave.

According to Dad, Barry has been messing around with some pretty stupid people, including the vacant plot, Catherine O'Conor. I only got to hear snatches, even though I kept saying to Dad that I was old enough to hear the truth. Tyler pulled me away and advised me to leave them alone. How could I have thought that Tyler was a snob, spoilt? Yes, he is beyond ordinary, but he's funny and kind.

Anyway, all this sad drama is like it all happened before, with Terry. Mum blamed herself completely for that mess. So did Dad. Then Tyler told me exactly what sort of real mess Barry had mired himself in. Barry had decided that he wanted to experiment with drugs. Do you make that decision? Today . . . Drugs . . . Anyway, some of the boys in school knew exactly where to go to get whatever he thought was a good idea at the time. Barry, who has a lot of spare cash, dealt with these boys quite a few times. No details as yet but, according to Tyler, Maud, who has to be one of the most peaceful people I know, almost thumped him. I know that she won't be bothered about what anyone thinks. She has rules which she feels are basic to all our requirements.

Whatever went wrong tonight, one of the boys decided to overcharge Barry, or underchange him. Barry flipped, threw a punch and . . . the rest is history. Dave and Toby appeared on the scene after about ten guys landed on top of Barry. I can feel another Dora ban coming on. Poor Dad was going on about how he had no control. But that isn't the point, Dad. Out there, when we're on our own, it's us who have to decide. Dad's genuinely tried; in fact I think that he's tried too hard, done too much thinking for us. Not that it matters now. Tyler. Please don't go in September. Having you around means I cope. Just. Get well soon, Dave.

✪ Thirty-five

Sunday 29th July . . . 4.48 pm.

Wimbledon has been and gone and I've just got back from playing tennis with Tyler, Amy and Terry. Initially, the first few times that we played, I was scared I'd look a fool. But Tyler makes me feel good about everything. Do I do that for him, make him special? Amy says that I'm sickening in love. Well, it's the first time and, in between being petrified that it will all be gone tomorrow, I think I'm coping pretty well.

Dave is still in dark glasses, insists that they have to be Ray Bans. Terry had a mechanic mate in the garage who got a pair of imitations for next to nothing. Dave's happy. The operation was a success. There is still a wait to make sure that everything will carry on healing but, so far, so good. The amazing thing was that it brought Billie and

Henry scuttling over – not for Dave, for Barry. According to Tyler, Christian, who rarely gets embroiled in the basics of his family, demanded that the parents speak to their son.

'He was brilliant,' Tyler told me.

'Did he get angry?' I can't see Christian angry.

'This wasn't anger, it was biblical. Wrath of God and all that.'

He does look a bit like an Old Testament picture without the beard.

'He blasted Billie for never condemning anything, always gazing into the distance and talking about spiritual experiences.'

That fitted.

It's amazing how bad things can turn out well. Just like you said, Granny L. Henry isn't anything like I imagined. It's odd the way you store up an image of someone and they turn out almost the opposite. For a start, he's a bit smaller than me. An immediate dilemma. I hate towering over my parents, I certainly didn't want to tower over Tyler's. I wanted to make a good impression. And he's got a shaved head. Dave was deeply impressed and insists that, before he starts at the new school, he too will shave his head.

There's so much to say. I can't write quickly enough. Dave has a place at St. Stephen's. The headmaster knew all about him, but good things; he had heard about Dave's intervention in the Barry fight. Dave, all 'I'm out to beat authority', is already in the new Head's good books, for 'foolhardy defence', as the Head called it, but 'sound principles'. Dave? Principles? I don't think so, but he does have a few good points. For example, when he saw the old tissue diary he asked me if next time I'd print my writing; he couldn't understand a word!!! I almost hugged him. Then, I hope he was teasing, he congratulated me on the Science book effort.

'Your writing's definitely improved.'

I wanted to bury him, but he's recovering, I let him off.

Jacob and Tina don't exist any more. They returned, poor abandoned lovers, as an unsolicited manuscript. Sally insists that all the best writers are rejected first time round. Maybe, then again, it was a nice dream, a good try, but not good enough. I've given it to Tyler, who insists that he'll find me a publisher, some day, some-where.

✨ Thirty-six

Tuesday 31st. Watch lost, again. Clock on the missing list. Today saw the arrival of our school reports. What can I say? Well, it was bad, but not as bad as it should have been. I failed French. That came as no surprise. But that was all. I even passed, just, Irish. Terry's was pretty much like mine and Dave was delighted to have a sheet of almost blank paper and a personal letter from Mr. Kennedy congratulating him on his new school. Hypocrite!

Dad muttered and mumbled about Ms. Wolfe.

'She's a first-class . . .'

'Robert.' Mum, raising her hand and pulling her lips together, looked almost autocratic.

'What is it between you two?' I asked, innocently.

Sean was out in the front, clearing weeds and chatting to Jen, who, following super-Belle's instructions, was lying around in a bikini.

'Nothing,' Dad said, looking into his coffee cup as if he'd found the secrets of the planet in the bottom.

'They went out together, Anna,' Mum explained, smiling.

'God.' Sick thought. The she-wolf might have been my mother. No. She'd never have taken on the kind of responsibility that Mum and Dad have.

'I wasn't good enough,' Dad explained.

Mum, smiling, looked up and then said, 'What you were was too good.'

Dad blushed. Happiness overload. I think that they are finally on the road to recovery.

◎ Thirty-seven

*T*his is it, parchment pages. I have waited and stored and waited, because I wanted to feel as if this last entry meant something. And it does. Today is Thursday the seventeenth of August. Exactly five months from the start of you, my diary. Downstairs there's a bit of a celebration going on. Tyler is lying on my bed. I want him to stay there forever, but forever isn't possible. In under three weeks he'll be gone. I can't think about that because it leaves a gap inside me that is unstoppable.

Mum talked to me the other day about love hurting, and love changing, and love crushing. We had a cry together. That felt not bad. It was as if she understood. And she does. All those secret changes that I've noticed do have a cause. She's pregnant. I was so angry, so furious that they could be so stupid. Six children is too many; they can't afford us. I told her. And she laughed.

'If we all thought about what we can afford we'd never have a single child.'

I was still angry.

'But this is a big surprise.'

You can say that again. Jen was meant to be the surprise that ended all surprises.

'We didn't mean for it to happen.'

Oh great, I thought. They, the do-gooders, the Margarets with their faeces and toxicaria and Weil's disease and teenage pregnancies, expect us in the Aids age to be careful. BUT, the older ones, my parents for God's Sake! Enough. I was and am still slightly horrified. And just after she'd lost all that weight. Sean thinks the whole thing is a miracle. He would. He's soft in the head.

Tyler and I haven't stopped talking about IT . . . the pregnancy. He reckons that I should be pleased and supportive. He also maintains that it's like a warning to us, him and me – it's that easy. Hey! Wait a minute, I wanted to say. There is no way, ever, that I would put somebody through what I've been through, little Lou-Lou will go through, Dr Morrison's adopted kids. We need to know where we come from. If . . . when I'm ready to sleep with someone, it's going to be because I have to imagine the possibility of creating somebody else. It has to be, because that is the way it might turn out. Tyler told me I was perfect. I can accept that.

I'll, we'll, have to go down in a minute. Mr. Eglinton has just yelled up the stairs that they're about to cut the cake. It's a replica of the shop and frosted on top is

166

FIELDING'S, Sally's handiwork. We beat him, we finally beat Mr. Arthur O'Conor. In three days time we move into the house and take over. Our shop, ours and Uncle Sean's. But there's more. Sean said that he needed another challenge, so he's also found himself a small bakery. It's a few miles away, old, tumbledown, but with health and safety cover as long as he makes a few changes. He intends to get people in to make sandwiches with home-made bread, take them round to businesses, buy vans – in the future. Sean can only see ahead. He keeps begging me not to look backward. I'm trying, Sean.

Tyler and I will go down in a minute. We both cry a bit thinking about being apart. I suppose I wish fast-forward, as usual. When I saw Polly and Liam a little while ago, they both told me to be happy for now. Andrew's here, with Olivia. God, I don't want to get married. There's too much else to do and see.

It's been good knowing you, book. Next term I'll have to find something new, inscrutable, different. Maybe an ordinary five-year diary, with lock!

'We're coming.'

Oh, but I loved the blank pages. I'm closing up for the last time, but nothing will make me forget what's scribbled on the cover from so long ago. Anna, 4ever friends, Amy xxx. And now Tyler's name is underneath the inscription, because he's just this minute put it there.